THE TALENT COU

There must be m. against the wind than she had seen with her untutored eye, but which now, in the light of Nathan's insight, would be clear to her. She could *feel* the power within herself, and knew that even a small fire would suffice. She settled with her back against a tree, legs folded in front of her, and threw the green stuff on to the flames. Resting her hands in her lap, she gazed into the smoke, watching it take shape.

It was as if she were there, on the deck of the great ship, as it heeled in the wind. Men ran to haul on ropes, the water gurgled over the side. There were birds, flying above the banked clouds of the sails. The vision was more real than it had ever been, and had come so quickly . . .

John Gribbin used to be a science writer, but wants to be a science fiction writer when he grows up. He is best known for his books about science which read like science fiction, especially *In Search of Schrödinger's Cat* and *In Search of the Edge of Time*. He has written (or co-written) six published SF novels to date, including *The Sixth Winter* and *Ragnarok*. He also presented the series *Science or Fiction?* on BBC World Service, and is a life member of Kent CCC.

INNERVISIONS

JOHN GRIBBIN

A ROC BOOK

PENGUIN BOOKS

Published by the Penguin Group
Penguin Books Ltd, 27 Wrights Lane, London W8 5TZ, England
Penguin Books USA Inc., 375 Hudson Street, New York, New York 10014, USA
Penguin Books Australia Ltd, Ringwood, Victoria, Australia
Penguin Books Canada Ltd, 10 Alcorn Avenue, Toronto, Ontario, Canada M4V 3B2
Penguin Books (NZ) Ltd, 182–190 Wairau Road, Auckland 10, New Zealand

Penguin Books Ltd, Registered Offices: Harmondsworth, Middlesex, England

First published by ROC, an imprint of Penguin Books 1993
1 3 5 7 9 10 8 6 4 2

Typeset by Datix International Limited, Bungay, Suffolk
Filmset in 10/12 pt Monophoto Melior and Ehrhardt
Printed in England by Clays Ltd, St Ives plc

For Ben Gribbin
with thanks for plot discussions and keyboard skills

PROLOGUE

In the depths of space, far from any star, the sphere floated in blackness. With no nearby reference point, it would have been hard for any outside observer to determine its size, or whether it was moving. Such an observer would, however, have noted the twelve smooth bulges, symmetrically placed about the surface of the sphere, and the network of lines connecting them. Along one of the lines a vehicle moved, seemingly with painful slowness. At another point on the sphere, far from any bulge or track, a machine seemed to be busy about some incomprehensible task. But, of course, there was no intelligent being around to notice any of this, far from any star.

ONE

Elyse woke from the dream slowly, with heavy lidded eyes that were reluctant to open, even though she knew she was awake. Her tongue felt thick in her dry mouth. Her neck ached. When the dreams came upon her, she seemed to waken more tired than when she had fallen into bed, if that were possible. And it was worse when the dream made no sense, just as this one had made no sense.

When she dreamed of the great ships, or the bird-men, or other strange people going about their incomprehensible tasks, at least she had the anchor of their obvious *peopleness* to cling on to. A dream about people, no matter how strange, and whatever strange business they were about, was at least in part related to the comforting familiarity of everyday life. But to dream of metal spiders, crawling about over a metal egg, floating in a black sea, surely carried the stamp of madness.

This dream, recur though it might, she would never reveal to anybody. But the others? How much could she, dare she, reveal to the Elders?

Her gift, if it were a gift and not a curse, was known to them already, thanks to her childish indiscretions. Now, on the threshold of womanhood, she knew better how to guard her tongue. But discretion had come too late to prevent the curiosity of the Elders from being roused, to prevent her being brought here, to the Halls, spared the heavy labour of the fields but treated no better than a serving-girl while being watched as closely as if she were, indeed, imprisoned. The Elders knew she had a Talent, but they did not know if it was for good or ill. And until they decided, Elyse would have no freedom.

Suddenly, breaking out of the spell cast by the dream, she sat up in bed, shrugging off the thin cover that was all she needed during the warm season, and hugged her knees, gazing out past the rough logs of the wall, through the window, at the hills beyond. Although nearly eighteen summers old, Elyse still had the figure of a young girl, her chest almost as flat as that of a boy. Her black hair scarcely reached to her shoulders; the dark eyes, wide in the face that, in spite of its freckles, was pale from the long hours she now spent indoors, were focused on nothing at all, as she pictured in her mind not the real hills outside the window but the ones where she had run as a child, freely, before the suspicion of her Talent grew into a certainty and she was sent by her parents into the care of the Elders.

If they decided that her Talent was not in the interests of the people, then before another summer came, she would be married. Bedded by a man chosen for her by the Elders from a bloodline rich, as far as any were, in Talents — but probably someone she would never meet before the wedding ceremony. She felt a fluttery queasiness in the pit of her stomach at the thought, like the scared but pleasurable feeling when she had, long ago, climbed to the top of a high tree where the light branches, swaying in the breeze, threatened to throw her to the ground at any minute. The prospect excited her physically even though she recoiled from it with her mind. For then, with her Talent gone, she would be free to leave the Halls, and return to the fields and hills outside. But free only to be the companion of a farmer, to help him tend the fields, to bear children who, if they were girls, would

4

be particularly carefully watched for any signs of burgeoning Talent.

And if the Elders approved of her Talent? If they found a way to turn it to advantage? Why, then she would become an Elder herself, one of the rulers of the people, a prospect as exciting mentally as the prospect of being paired with a man affected her body. But as an Elder, she would be for ever a prisoner of the Halls, obedient to their forms and customs, using her Talent for the good of all, kept locked away like a precious work of art, and never to feel the touch of a man − never, indeed, to be alone with a man.

The one certainty in the road mapped out for her when she entered the Halls at the age of fourteen was that, one way or the other, she would never be free to travel the Land alone, to run where she liked across the hills, accountable to nobody but herself. And that, of course, was the one thing that Elyse craved above all else.

There was certainly plenty of Land to travel, for those with the inclination and the freedom to do so. From the Halls, set back from the shore by the side of the Little River, you could ride for four days in either direction, eastward to the Great River or west, to where the mountains came down to the sea, and never leave the dominion of the Elders. Inland, the region of settled farms and coppiced woodlands extended all the way to the White Mountains, where gentle hills shaded into the sheer, unclimbable cliffs, shrouded in the cloud that gave them their name, that reached up to unimaginable mysteries beyond. And both to east and to west, beyond the Great River and the coastal mountains, there were further settlements, accessible only by the small vessels that plied the coastal waters. These owed nominal allegiance to the Elders, but were rumoured to be the homes of wild Talents and strange, barbaric practices. Beyond them lay the wilderness itself; but even so adventurous a spirit as Elyse recoiled from the thought of ever going *that* far.

The outer villages, though. She could day-dream if nothing else, of finding a home there, concealing her Talent, and leading a normal life. Or even, if the stories were true, of using her Talent, an important person in a small community, not just one very junior Elder among many, free from the forms and customs of the Halls. That was the most exciting prospect of all both to mind and body − even if it was the least likely to come to fruition, and even if she still had no idea, after four years of Dreaming, of what use her Talent might be to anybody at all, if it was indeed a true Talent.

But neither Dreaming nor day-dreaming could keep her from her duties as a probationer in the Halls. And the great bell, tolled by the sister probationer on duty by the water-clock, said that it was already the seventh hour. Hurriedly, Elyse slid off the bed and washed the remaining sleep out of her eyes. Slipping out of her nightdress, she pulled on undergarments, and then the ankle-length, high-necked blue gown with white collar and cuffs. It would be over-warm in the summer heat, but modesty was more important than comfort in the Halls. It would never do for any man to be excited by the sight of even a probationary Elder. Though Elyse thought, not for the first time, as she ran her hands down her slim body to smooth the gown into place, that there was precious little chance of any man even noticing that she was more than a child, except for her height. She ran her fingers through her hair, not bothering with a comb, and hurried from the room. Kitchen duty first − waiting at table on the Elders, clearing away, washing up, and only then would she be allowed her own morning meal. No time to lose.

6

Sitting at the rough table in the kitchen hall, she watched the dying embers of the cooking fire as she mechanically shovelled the last of the porridge from the wooden bowl into her mouth. The thin coil of grey smoke, rising from the bed of the fire, seemed to take on the shapes of her dreams, puffing out like the fat sails of the ships of her imagination. Automatically, she pushed a stray strand of hair out of her eyes with her free hand, while the hand holding the spoon stopped moving. Perhaps it was just imagination. Or perhaps not. Just how the Elders expressed their own Talents was a carefully guarded secret. Each probationer had to find her own path to the truth. But there were stories of sisters who could shape clouds to their will, or who made the branches of living trees move to their whim. Would it be so strange if her Talent, gaining strength from her dreams, were now to be manifested in the control of fire smoke? And did it mean she was ready at last to be Tested?

She would *never* be ready to be Tested. Pulling her eyes away from the fire and its smoke, Elyse looked about her. Lifting the spoon to her lips, she licked the last traces of porridge from its surface. At least the food was plentiful here, and good, if plain. The Elders said that too much pandering to the weakness of the body made it soft, and thereby weakened the spirit. But no Talent could function properly if the body it chose to occupy was not healthy and strong.

Only the two youngest probationers were at the table with her. They treated Elyse, the oldest probationer, with almost as much deference as they gave the Elders, and had made no attempt to interrupt her reverie, whispering quietly to each other as they completed their simple meal. There were only six probationers in all; soon, one way or the other, there would be only five. Nobody could become an Elder before the age of sixteen; nobody could stay a probationer beyond the age of eighteen. Time was closing in on Elyse. She could feel the change coming over her, the power of her Talent growing within. A Talent to control smoke; to see visions not just in her dreams, but in the coils of writhing grey given up by the living wood in its fiery death throes. But would she be able to control those visions? And would they be able to tell her of things of value to the people? Or would she still only see strange lands, strange ships, and even stranger metal eggs and spiders?

Karyn, slightly the elder of the two children on the opposite side of the table, glanced up at Elyse, half smiled, then ducked her head as if concentrating on her now empty bowl. Elyse smiled in return, remembering when she had been like them, new to the Halls, nervous but excited, wondering what it would be like to be an Elder, still not sure whether or not she really was the bearer of a Talent herself.

'Well, Karyn. If you scrape much longer at that bowl, you'll wear a hole in it. What duties do you have this morning, that keep you so long at the table?'

The child looked up again, and blushed. Her companion, Miryam, giggled.

'Oh, please, Elyse . . . we have lessons, until the midday bell.'

'Then perhaps you should hurry along to Sister Tutor, while there are still a few moments left before the bell.' She reached across the table for their bowls and spoons. 'I will attend to these.'

'Yes, Elyse.' The two small figures pushed back their bench, and hurried away, still giggling. Maybe she would have been more at home here, Elyse briefly thought, if she had entered with a companion her own age. But it hadn't happened that way. There had only been four other girls, all much older than her, one of whom, once called Marretta, was now Sister Tutor. Her chosen name, like those of the other Elders, reflected her Talent. A gift for communication, for imparting knowledge, and maybe even wisdom; clearly, a Talent of great value to the people.

And little Karyn, what name would she take? It was easy for her to be so happy, who had such an obvious Talent so young. Since Karyn had been ten years old, her father's farm had been the talk first of his village, then of the Eastern Settlements, and then of the whole people. The crops that little Karyn tended grew tall and straight, free from any blight; the animals she fed never took sick. Sister Green, that would suit her. And surely she would be taking her name as soon as she was of age, at sixteen summers. While Elyse, already nearly eighteen, still awaited a decision and a name. A useless Talent at best; a talent for seeing pictures in the grey of wood-smoke. Sister Grey, that would suit her, she thought bitterly, the smile vanishing from her lips. If not Mistress Grey.

She pushed her own bench back and picked up the utensils. Might as well get used to a life of chores and drudgery.

※　　※　　※

It was unreasonably hot for the time of day. The sun beat straight down on Rantor's head from the zenith with scarcely any protecting cloud layer, even though it would soon be night. Pausing in his purposeful march to the shipyard he pulled a large kerchief from the leather pouch on his belt and mopped first his forehead, then the back of his neck. Wadding the cloth in his right hand as he prepared to put it away, he glanced up at the four flag-poles on the high tower of the castle at the head of the bay. Sure enough, three of the poles were bare, while on the fourth a single flag flapped limply at half-mast in the unusually weak sea breeze. More than half-way through the fourth quarter; dark in less than two candles. And hardly a cloud overhead. Freak winds. Nothing to worry about, just one of those things. But where would a sailor be if he couldn't depend on the sea breeze by day and the land breeze by night?

Rantor shivered at the thought, in spite of the heat. The reliable winds provided the only sure means of navigation around the Archipelago. Which was why it was worth following up any lead that might provide a means to navigate beyond the Archipelago, out in the broad ocean. Even a lead as half-baked as the mission he was now on. Once again, he stepped out briskly towards the yard, the small shadow cast by the almost unbearably bright pinpoint of light overhead flickering beneath him as he strode along.

It had begun several fivedays before with a summons from his Lord, Kyper, the most powerful man in the Three Islands, perhaps the most powerful in the entire Archipelago, though that was not to say that the concerted efforts of three or more of his rivals might not bring about his embarrassment. Which was the reason why much of Lord Kyper's resources were devoted to ensuring that it never occurred to those rivals to work in union against him – and why most of the rest of those resources were spent in seeking ways to consolidate his own position. Since Kyper was no fool, that meant most of the inhabitants of the Three Islands were well cared for, and that their Lord's justice, while swift, was also accurate. To be in the service of Kyper himself was as much as any mortal inhabitant of the Archipelago could hope for. But even the most loyal and trusted servant, the Navigator himself, still felt a *frisson* of fear at any sudden summons from the castle.

The greeting had, however, been cordial enough, with just the minimum of formality that protocol required in the presence of a third party. A stranger to Rantor, and an outlander as well by the cut of his clothes.

'Well, Navigator.' The Duke seemed pleased, and reinforced his greeting with a brotherly embrace, both hands gripping Rantor's shoulders, not just the right as courtesy demanded. Kyper was still an impressive figure; fit, though slightly overweight, with just a touch of grey at the temples and speckling the black of his beard.

'I have a new fool, as you can see.' His left hand swept out to indicate the odd-looking figure, while his right hand slid naturally across Rantor's shoulder. The stranger could have been left in no doubt that Rantor was the Duke's most trusted aide and companion – which was certainly news to Rantor. But if this was the way my Lord Kyper wanted to play the scene, then so be it.

'Indeed? He seems none too amusing to me.'

'Ah, but this fool's appearance is deceptive. He looks ordinary enough. But he has ambition: to sail to the edge of the world.'

Rantor looked more closely at the little man. A lunatic? There must be more to this story than that, or the Duke would not be taking this personal interest. Rantor had no illusions about his supposed friendship with Lord Kyper, but the Duke knew the value of a good Navigator, and wouldn't waste time with idle jests.

The man was clearly nervous, but not overawed by his surroundings. He seemed determined enough in spite of his slight stoop and forward-tilted head. He looked sharply at the two of them, almost like a cat sizing up a rival.

'My Lord'. He spoke softly but firmly, like a patient tutor with a difficult child.

'I know that you like to jest. But your guest may not appreciate the joke. If this is your famous Navigator, please do not make him think that I am an idiot. I do not seek to *find* the edge of the world. I merely suggested that there must be an edge.'

Startled by the discourteous way in which the stranger treated the Duke as an equal, Rantor looked to Lord Kyper for guidance. The Duke half smiled, and raised an eyebrow. Clearly, madman or fool, the stranger was being given as much licence as an official jester. But – the edge of the world? There lay madness indeed, since every schoolboy knew that the world beyond the Archipelago was infinite and unchanging, a flat ocean that spread equally in all directions.

The Duke spoke, moving aside to a table as he did so. 'This disrespectful outlander is called Hawk. Not for his physical attributes, you understand, but because, like a soaring bird, he sees further than the rest. I have evidence of his peculiar skills, or he would not be with us now.' He turned to the stooping man. Yes, thought Rantor, his eye is more like that of an eagle or a hawk than a cat.

'And this, my friend Hawk,' the ironic emphasis on the word *friend* could not be mistaken, 'is indeed Rantor, the

12

greatest navigator in the Three Islands, and doubtless therefore the best in all the Archipelago. Convince him that there is more than madness in your schemes and my patronage is assured.'

Hawk's manner changed, becoming politely more subservient as he turned his attentions to the Navigator. Rantor realized that this came hard to the small man, who clearly was not used to pretending subservience to anyone. He must care deeply about the need to enlist the Navigator in his cause; Rantor was more impressed by this than by the words themselves.

'Navigator, I apologize for my rudeness. I come from a far island, and I am not used to civilized ways. Also I have spent a long time, and much effort, to reach the ear of the only man who can help me fulfil my dream.' Did he mean the Duke? Or himself? Rantor pondered. The Duke was all powerful here. Yet if the Hawk wished to venture out into the wide ocean, even the Duke could not help him without the Navigator's approval . . .

'It is true, I believe – for very good reasons, I assure you – that our world is finite. But I also believe there is more to our world than an Archipelago.'

Ah! the Many Worlds heresy. That explained the interest of the Duke – and why there were no observers present at the meeting.

'But surely, Hawk, we are taught that there is only one Archipelago, set by God in the midst of the eternal ocean. If our Lord were not so generously disposed to his guests, you could find yourself in some discomfort for voicing such heresies.'

The Duke smiled. 'All are free to speak their mind in my domain, Navigator, as well you know.' And the Duke's domain extended, as Rantor also well knew, only as far as the rule of his arms and the loyalty of his followers. There were priests who ostensibly owed allegiance to the Duke, but who would undoubtedly take action against an outspoken heretic, especially an outlander. Even Lord Kyper lacked the power to change the laws on religious matters, in the face of a church which might be subservient in the administration of the Three Islands, but which extended its tentacles throughout the Archipelago, and didn't lack for fanatical followers. It was a wonder this fellow had lived to find his way to the comparative freedom of the Duke's realm.

'My Lord Kyper is indeed a generous host, as well as one possessed of a distinctive sense of humour. He is also aware, Navigator, that if there is any truth in these heresies, then somebody stands to benefit by it. I have no interest in wealth for myself. As a means to an end, of course, I appreciate its value. But my interest lies in finding out new things, questioning old beliefs, and investigating the world in which we live with an open mind. A Navigator such as yourself, whose fame has spread across the Archipelago, must surely share some of those feelings.'

'Perhaps.' He looked to the Duke for approval, and took his slight nod as encouragement to continue.

'I have sailed out of sight of even the farthest islands, and I have seen floating branches and flying birds that might – I only say might – have come from beyond the Archipelago. But to go in search of other islands, other archipelagos, with no safe means of return,' he shrugged, 'is more than any competent Navigator would risk.'

'But suppose there was no risk?' Now they were getting to the point of the meeting. In spite of himself, Rantor felt a stirring of hope in his breast. It was every navigator's dream, and although the chance of its being achieved was tiny the fruits of the success would be so sweet that any possibility had to be explored.

He was yet young, and he had achieved a great deal. As

much as anyone in his profession could achieve. Navigator to the Duke Kyper. What more could he ask? And yet, a restlessness burned within him still, a longing for something – he knew not what. But something, to be sure, that could not be found in the Archipelago, for he had sailed the length and breadth of these islands and had yet to find the thing that would give him peace.

'You have a way of navigating beyond the Archipelago?' He made it a question, as desperate not to allow himself to be taken in by any false hopes as he was eager to find those hopes fulfilled. But the little man they called the Hawk had clearly been able to spot, immediately, the true response of the Navigator to even the hint of such an achievement.

It was his turn to smile. 'A Navigator, indeed. We both want the same thing, if for different reasons. And we can both serve our noble Lord well, while following our own dreams. Yes, Navigator Rantor, I have a means to sail beyond the Archipelago, and find our way back again. How far we can sail, and what we might find, only God can say.' The smile suggested that Hawk trusted more in the ability of himself and a human Navigator than in the whim of God. 'But I am sure the journey will be worth while, and with our Lord's permission I will explain.'

The Duke nodded. 'With the understanding, Navigator, that none of this passes your lips outside these walls.'

TWO

Instead of sitting demurely on the hard wooden bench outside Sister Senior's room, Elyse knelt, the wood painfully pressing on her thin knees, so that she could look out of the window, craning her neck to gaze at the grey clouds rolling overhead. Why was Sister Senior so interested in clouds?

The Testing had not been anything like she had expected. Sister Senior and her two companions had been far less terrifying than the ordeal Elyse had imagined. They had *wanted* her to pass the Test, to show that she had some Talent of use to the people. Well, of course they had. They wanted more Talents, to replace the elderly Sisters. The community in the Halls was small enough, anyone could see that. But anyone could also see that the Testing had to be severe, to ensure that only Sisters with genuinely valuable Talents stayed in the Halls. A useless Talent, no matter how interesting, was better sacrificed to the next generation, in the hope that the daughters of the failed probationer might prove of greater value to the people. After all, where else would the next generation of Talents come from?

So the Testing had to be severe. It had to be an ordeal, no matter how much Sister Senior might want to expand the sisterhood itself. Nothing that Elyse had heard had prepared her for the possibility that the Sisters might be not just eager, but almost *desperate* to find some hidden usefulness in her pathetic Talent. Of course, that had not been said, nor had they even hinted as much. But some-

But fulfilment of expectation did nothing to dull the disappointment she felt as she walked alongside Sister Senior, out of the Halls proper, across the dusty courtyard under the grey sky to the visitors' quarters. The single-storey wooden building, no more than two rooms, lay alongside the tall fence, close by the gate. The flow of words went past her unheeded as they walked – something about her duty to the people, raising daughters who might take her place in the Halls after all, that she would always have an honoured place among the people.

The flow of words stopped at the entrance to the small building. Sister Senior held out both her hands to Elyse, took her by the shoulders, kissed her lightly on each cheek.

'Goodbye, child.'

She was gone, leaving Elyse on the threshold of the quarters, where a young guard stood grinning at her. He opened the door, bowed low, then spoke.

'Don't take it too hard, girl. There's more to life than the Halls, as you'll soon see. And if you don't like the farmer's boy they've picked out for you, just come back here and ask for Rafe. I'll show you a better time than any of those old Sisters have ever seen!'

Furious, cheeks red, she swept into the room and flung the door shut behind her before he could offer further help. So soon! Still within the fence, although technically not quite in the Halls, and her changed status was flung at her like this. Not that Rafe would dream of touching her – life as a Halls guard was too good to risk, even though it was only his job, not his life, that he would lose for molesting a mere failed probationer. But if she were still even a probationer, let alone a Sister, such comments would never have passed his lips. So much for the modest dress and her slender figure!

She sat down hard on the narrow bed under the

window, catching her breath, calming her racing thoughts. What chance would she get, now, to find out more about her Talent? Within a week, she would be wed. Until then, she would be a prisoner in this place, with nobody except the guard to talk to. And after the wedding night, it would be too late.

She heard the bell sound twice while she sat, unmoving, unthinking, on the bed. Somewhere in the back of her mind she was aware that she had not eaten, and that it would soon be dark. But what did it matter? Her life was no longer her own; she would wait for someone to tell her what to do, where to go, who to marry. Nothing else had any reality for her now.

The light knock at the door seemed at first to be nothing to do with her, either. But when it was repeated, a little louder, she stirred at last.

'Come in.'

It was Karyn. Little Karyn, the most junior of the probationers, clutching a bundle of what could only be Elyse's few clothes. They might at least have sent someone more her own age, that she could talk to. Maybe this was some Sister's idea of putting her in her place, sending only the most junior member of the Halls on a distasteful errand. Or maybe it was some kind of pointed comment on her own pathetic Talent, sending the girl with the most useful Talent seen in the Halls for a generation. But whatever message the Sisters might be trying to convey, the blame couldn't be laid on Karyn herself, who stood, looking about her nervously, in the doorway. She was only a child, and secure in her Talent. What could she know of Elyse's loss?

'Come in,' she repeated, more warmly. 'You've got my things?'

She nodded, moving forward and dumping the bundle on the bed as Elyse stood to make room. 'Everything from your trunk. Clothes. Brushes and things. Some ornaments.'

Elyse laughed. Well, there was one advantage of leaving the Halls. She could wear the pretty pins and rings that she had had to put away when she became a probationer.

On impulse, she opened the bundle, found the small leather bag that contained her trinkets, tipped its contents out on the bed. There was a small copper-coloured ring, two strands of metal twisted around one another, her favourite when she too had been a child. She held it out to Karyn.

'Would you like this one? Perhaps it will remind you of me, when you are Sister Senior and I am an old woman with hundreds of grandchildren.'

Karyn looked uncertain.

'Oh, it's all right, you know. The rules say you mustn't *display* ornamentation. Everybody keeps a few pretty things of their own, to look at in private.'

The child took the ring, and returned the smile.

'And when your granddaughters come into the Halls, I'll show it to them and tell them who gave it to me! It really won't be too bad, Elyse. I'm sorry you can't stay with us. But I used to like the farm. I expect you will, too. There's lots to do there, and places to go, and . . .'

'Not so many places for the mistress of the house to go, I don't suppose. The kitchen, the dairy, the washroom. Not much time to run in the fields, or climb trees.'

The child was crestfallen, pathetically eager to help Elyse to look on the brighter side.

'But Sister Senior said –' She stopped, turning slightly to one side, and half raising a hand to her mouth. It was the action, as much as the words, that alerted Elyse.

'Sister Senior? Did she send you on this errand?'

Karyn nodded.

Elyse pushed the small heap of her possessions to one side, making room for them both on the bed. Taking Karyn by the hand, she made her sit beside her.

'And she told you to cheer me up by telling me about life on the farm? Is that it?'

The child nodded again.

Anger grew in Elyse's breast. She knew her duty, and understood her fate. She didn't need some innocent child persuading her that life on the farm was wonderful. She knew it wasn't, and she would do it anyway – but it hurt that Sister Senior thought so little of her that she would seek to persuade her in this way.

A spark of rebellion burned inside her. If they thought she was so unworthy, why should she really bother about what they wanted? What difference would it really make, breeding daughters with stupid Talents like her own, of no use to anybody? What if she *could* walk in the fields, and climb the trees, once again? But she would have to get far, far away from the Halls first.

She put her arm around Karyn.

'Perhaps Sister Senior is right. I do need someone to remind me how good life can be outside. After all, I've been in here for four years, and I don't remember much about anything else. You come from the Eastern Settlements, don't you?'

'Yes, Elyse.'

'A long journey.'

'I came in a boat!' The girl's eyes grew big at the memory. 'It took five days!'

'Tell me about it, Karyn, please. Tell me about the farm, and all the people in your village. And your special friends. They must have been very proud, when you were chosen for the Halls?'

'Oh yes. There was a feast. Everybody came – except Gregor.' Her eyes lost their sparkle.

'Gregor?'

'My brother. Much older than me.' Karyn sighed, then

22

smiled at some happy memory. 'He used to call me his favourite girl. Sometimes he let me work the bellows for him. He said I could be the first lady smith in the Settlements, when he got too old and feeble to carry on.' The smile vanished. 'He didn't want me to go. He said it was a waste, sending me away. He said I could use my Talent right there, in the village, just as I always had. But he was wrong, wasn't he, Elyse?'

She turned to the older girl for comfort, looking up at her, seeking reassurance. Their roles were hardly being played out in the way Sister Senior must have planned.

Elyse nodded. 'Of course. You did the right thing. In the Halls, your Talent can be trained, developed to help everybody, not just one village. I expect your brother realizes that, now. And with your particular Talent, as soon as you are of age you're bound to go back out into the Settlements. You'll be seeing Gregor again by the time you are as old as me. Maybe you'll see me, too, somewhere out there. Tell me about your journey. I was born near here, you know, by the side of the Little River. I've never even seen the Great River, let alone the Eastern Settlements.'

But, she thought, as Karyn settled into her tale, there's a first time for everything. Elyse listened attentively to the story, mentioning names of people and places. If nothing else, that ability was one thing she would take with her thanks to her years of study in the Halls, under the guidance of Sister Tutor and her predecessor. She knew she had been a good pupil, in spite of the uselessness of her Talent. And anybody with the training of the Halls, and even a smattering of Talent, ought to be able to make do as a wise woman, somewhere out there, far from the influence of the Sisters . . .

※　　　※　　　※

Since the first time that the Hawk had outlined his strange ideas to the Navigator, he had in many conversations elaborated his dreams and his plans, until Rantor came almost to believe in them himself, just as he had grown to like the little man and to admire him for his strange genius. Whatever came out of this mission, he was sure, the Three Islands would never be the same again.

But still, the ideas were so strange; and having no one to discuss them with except the Hawk, who had utter faith in his own beliefs, Rantor sometimes wondered if there might be flaws he lacked the wit to perceive, or whether he really understood at all. He'd give a lot to discuss the strange philosophy with a sympathetic priest – but pick the wrong priest to open his mouth to, and the price might be his life. Instead, lacking anyone to confide in but himself, he rehearsed the Hawk's strange image of the world in his mind, as he headed briskly for the workshop where, if all went well, he would see proof of this man's genius at work.

As a Navigator, Rantor knew his geometry and trigonometry. From his own experience, not just the word of the priests or of the books they kept so closely to themselves, he knew that the sun did indeed shine down vertically on every island in the Archipelago. Of course, he had never felt any inclination to make measurements, but all his own experience told him that when the priests – or Hawk – said that those measurements always showed the sun to be precisely at the zenith, they were speaking truly. An ordinary man might have trouble grasping the implication, but Rantor understood the nature of parallel lines. Parallel lines meet only at infinity. If the sun were any reasonable distance above the flat plane of the world, then careful measurements and triangulation, the same techniques used in navigation, would reveal its height above the islands. For it always to appear vertically above any spot in the Archipelago, it must lie at an infinite height above the flat world. So much was clear. But what else could be inferred from the observation?

He smiled to himself as he recalled the one occasion that he had – almost – discomfited Hawk with his navigational skills. Few people could think in terms of three dimensions, living, as they did, on a flat plane. But the Navigator had always enjoyed abstract mathematics. As he had pointed out to Hawk, some philosophers had noted that the sun *could* appear vertically above every point on the world if the world formed the inner surface of a hollow sphere, with the sun at its centre. For a moment, even Hawk had been at a loss for words, struck by a novel concept. At least the mathematicians of the Three Islands had some tricks they could teach him! But then, his mind bright as ever, he had spotted the flaws in the argument with impressive speed. If the world were round, the Archipelago was lying at the bottom of the equivalent of a huge shallow valley. All the waters of the world would pour downwards, flooding the islands completely. The sun itself would fall from the sky, following the natural tendency of things to seek the lowest point. It was merely a pretty piece of geometry, no more practical in its applications than Artemis's theorem of prime numbers, no more meaningful than the negative square root of a quadratic equation; a clever parlour trick.

Indeed, the sun *must* be at infinite distance if this were the only alternative! A beautiful example of the doctrine of the absurd alternative – if two alternatives purported to resolve the same problem, but one 'solution' was clearly absurd, then

25

the second, however unlikely it might seem in everyday terms, must be the correct solution.

The priests taught, of course, that the world itself must also be infinite in extent, a flat plane extending externally in all directions, a featureless ocean surrounding the Archipelago. Logic then dictated that there must be only one Archipelago, created by God as a home for man. In an infinite ocean, there could in principle exist an infinite number of Archipelagos, with infinite varieties of life upon them. This was clearly absurd. So the logicians argued that there must either be many worlds, or that the Archipelago was unique – since the fact of their existence proved the Archipelago to be real, even to philosophers. If there were infinite numbers of archipelagos, many worlds, man would occupy no special place in creation, and could not represent God's work. So, the priests reasoned, there was only one Archipelago. Only heretics argued otherwise.

But Hawk claimed that the lights seen in the night sky from time to time were other worlds, like the world of the Archipelago. If so, they could not be infinite in extent, for if they were, either they would fill the sky and block out the light of the sun, or their infinite planes would intersect the plane of the world. If they were finite worlds, islands in the sky, then the world of the Archipelago might also be finite. And in a finite ocean there might exist a finite number of archipelagos, without running into the problems with infinites that plagued philosophers and tipped reasonable speculation into heresy.

Rantor shook his head, muttering wordlessly to himself as he strode along. To the Hawk, it seemed clear that an intersection of infinite worlds would be obvious to the inhabitants of the Archipelago; but the Navigator was not sure. In an infinite world, an infinite number of other worlds could intersect its plane, and still the nearest intersection might be infinitely far away from the Archipelago. And if the lights were other worlds, what stopped them falling on to the world? The sun might well be falling. At infinite distance, it could fall for ever and still get no closer to the Archipelago. But other worlds – finite worlds – floating like saucers in the sky?

The thought made his head spin. He pushed it to one side. Besides it was of no practical importance. Nobody suggested they might voyage to the worlds of those lights in the sky! Hawk's plan was crazy, but not that crazy. If the priests were wrong about the infinite extent of the world, Hawk argued, then they might be wrong in teaching that there was only one Archipelago. The fact that the Archipelago existed proved that there were islands, and life, in the world. And if one Archipelago could exist, why not others? The other worlds Hawk sought were only (only!) other archipelagos existing on the flat ocean of the world.

Rantor had doubts about the argument, though he was willing to take a reasonable risk on the off chance of finding new islands to trade with. He was also more than willing to follow up any prospect of a technique to navigate out of sight of land, out of feel of the sea breeze, and land breeze, and to find his way back, not just to the Archipelago but to any island of his choice, infallibly. It would make his master, the Duke, rich beyond compare, and some of the riches would rub off on him. And it would render established patterns of naval warfare obsolete overnight. If it worked.

Darkness came with its usual suddenness, although a few smoky torches had been lit in anticipation. The night glow, though something less than full darkness, such as you would experience in a closed room, was hardly sufficient light for any human being to see more than the vague shadows of buildings. Just ahead, the workshop that had been given over to the Hawk and his works stood out from its surroundings, lit up by the experimental gas lanterns that enabled the

Hawk to work such long hours, and were the reason why he had been allocated that particular building for his efforts. Rantor frowned slightly at the sight. To someone who depended on the safety of a wooden-walled ship for his trade – and his life – fire was a mixed blessing. Wooden houses and warehouses were scarcely any less at risk. To be sure, the Duke's artisans had been ingenious in devising this practical use of manure from the farms and from the earth closets of the town. But if they were to light more than a few buildings with the natural gas there would be no fertilizer left for the fields. No, gas lighting would remain a trick used only for special needs. And special needs, on the Archipelago, generally involved ships. Somewhere, somehow, some no good would come of this gas, Rantor was sure. But in the meantime, it meant he could attend Hawk's discreet demonstration at a time when most law-abiding citizens were at home, or at least safely shut away in some comforting tavern. When the sun went out, it was far too dark to be wandering the streets.

Just before he entered the building, the Navigator paused, shading his eyes and looking upward into the blackness, seeking a glimpse of the lights which Hawk set such store by. Of course, it was useless, His eyes were not dark-adapted, and even under ideal conditions, from the deck of a ship at sea, the lights never showed as more than a dim phosphorescence against the all-embracing blackness of the sky.

Hawk was waiting for him, impatiently tinkering with the complex apparatus that spilled over two tables and out on to the floor at one end of the long gallery. His two assistants stood nervously to one side. Armed guards, Rantor knew, filled the building. But all that mattered was Hawk himself and his strange experiment.

The tinkering stopped. 'You are alone, Navigator?'

'Who else did you expect?'

'I thought . . . but . . .'

Rantor smiled. 'I have the authority, Hawk, never fear. Persuade me that your trick works, and our Lord will not gainsay my decision. He would not risk a valuable ship on such an errand without his best Navigator, but if the Navigator approves, then the ship sails.'

'I suppose that's good.' The Hawk's sharp mind had instantly appraised that situation. 'Our Lord Kyper is an intelligent man, but he is an administrator, a soldier. It should be easier to make a practical man like you understand, and then . . .' His voice tailed off. So much of his life had been leading up to this moment that the Hawk, for all his wit, clearly had little or no idea what would happen next. He would be in the hands of the Navigator, embarking on a voyage into the unknown.

'Well, this is it.' He gestured at the complex web of apparatus. 'Don't worry about the details. Just watch.' He nodded at the assistants, one of whom promptly moved to a bank of large glass jars, and stood poised to turn what looked like a small capstan.

Hawk continued to talk. 'At this end of the room, we make artificial lightning. It's been done before but not on this scale. But down there,' he pointed along the gallery, 'is something completely new, the sensor. When we make lightning here,' pointing back to the main bank of apparatus, 'the sensor responds. Come with me and see.'

Following Hawk's lead, Rantor walked along the gallery. The sensor seemed a lot simpler than the lightning machine, which was just as well, since this was the equipment he was supposed to take to sea. The most prominent feature was a pair of metal spheres, about a thumb in diameter, almost touching one another. The whole apparatus, lightning machine and sensor, seemed, Rantor realized, incredibly profligate with metal. The value of the equipment would be more than the value of his own ship. The extent of the Duke's commitment, and the implications of failure after such an investment, seemed to cause a pricking of the hair at the back of his neck.

'Perhaps you can feel the lightning in the air.' So it wasn't fear! The Navigator smiled at his own foolishness.

'We can begin. Watch the gap between the two spheres.'

Hawk raised his right hand, and let it fall in a dramatic, clearly prearranged, signal to his assistants. At the far end of the gallery, one of them began to turn the small capstan. Immediately there was a crack, like thunder. In spite of Hawk's injunction, Rantor looked towards the sound at the far end of the room. A flash, like lightning, accompanied another thunderous crack, clearly somehow controlled by the turning of the wheel. Remembering his instructions, Rantor turned back to the apparatus before him. As the thunder continued, each crack was accompanied by tiny sparks leaping across the gap between the two spheres. The lightning at the far end of the gallery was being reproduced, in miniature, at the sensor!

Hawk raised his hand again; the noise, and the flashes, stopped. He shrugged. 'We can only keep it up for a short time, with this equipment. But the full-scale apparatus will be more effective.'

'This is just a model?'

'Of course. I'm planning to build the real thing in the castle, high up. With your approval, and Duke Kyper's permission, of course.'

'But how does it work?'

'The details are not important. It has to do with what I call the law of similarities. You will see that the construction of the sensor follows the pattern of the lightning generator. The morphology is crucial. When the lightning surges in the generator, there is a resonance in the sensor. The construction must be perfect, but when it is, we have the effect you see. I call it morphic resonance.'

Rantor was intrigued. He studied the strange shapes of the small machine before him, then walked along the gallery to compare the image in his mind with the structure of the lightning generator itself.

'And that is all?'

'Not quite all. The sensor could not respond at a distance, even if it were a perfect resonator, without being primed. When set to receive, the resonant sensor is in a state where it is almost ready to make its own sparks of lightning, spontaneously. It has the potentiality to make sparks. The resonance does no more than tip the balance.'

Rantor paid little attention to the words. As his initial surprise receded, he began to concentrate on the practicalities that concerned him.

'An impressive trick, Hawk. Everything you promised. Our Lord will be pleased. But how do you intend to use the trick in navigation?'

The little man smiled. 'It's wonderfully simple, Navigator. In my studies in my home island, before – well before . . .' Just how and why Hawk had left his home Rantor had yet to discover, though it was natural that anyone with a scheme to make money would gravitate to the Three Islands and the court of Duke Kyper. '. . . I worked on an even smaller scale than you see here, but I discovered a curious thing, a way to shield the resonator from the lightning. A metal screen – it need not be solid metal, just a mesh – placed between the generator and the sensor prevents the resonance. Now, it seems to me that a Navigator on a ship at sea, equipped with a resonator and a screen, need only move the screen around to find out on which side of the sensor it blocks the lightning. And that must be the direction the resonance is coming from – the way home!'

He stopped triumphantly. Rantor thought; he was less impressed than, it seemed, the Hawk expected. It might work.

Of course, it would be different, on the heaving deck of a ship, out of sight of land. But, yes, it might work. You could even rig a little circular track, for a truck like the ones used by the shipwrights in the yards, with the screen mounted on it. With stout hands at the ropes, and a good pulley system, you could run the shield around from place to place – well, no doubt any competent captain could attend to such details.

'Metal stops the, ah, resonance, you say?'

Hawk nodded.

'But not stone?'

'No, no effect at all.'

'So we can keep the generator securely shut away from prying eyes. Is there any limit to the resonance?'

Hawk shrugged. 'That is for us to find out. Before I came here, with a smaller model, the sensor worked at a distance of seven hundred paces, through several intervening houses. At sea – over greater distances – who knows?'

'But even if it works as you hope, how long can the generator operate? How can the Navigator at sea be sure to be seeking the signal at the right time?'

'A simple matter. We choose a time that cannot be mistaken – dawn perhaps. Every day at dawn, the generator runs for as long as possible. Every day at dawn the Navigator has his bearing. All he has to do is hold a true course through the day.'

The Navigator smiled. An easy enough task, said quickly. It almost made you wonder why the dukes and lords bothered to cosset their Navigators so. In fact, it would tax his skills to the utmost to make effective use of this trick. Which, to be sure, was one reason why he found the prospect so appealing.

Rantor was used to making decisions, and acting on them. He clapped Hawk on the shoulder.

'We will find out, Hawk, just how simple a task it proves. The Duke has put a new ship, the *Far Trader*, at my disposal.

A two-decker sixty paces long. You can get your sensor aboard tomorrow I trust? And then we'll see what it can do.'

'Tomorrow! Why, we can start now – my assistants know what to do –'

'And can they see in the dark like cats?' Rantor laughed. 'Tomorrow will do, my friend; but meanwhile, I know an inn, indeed more than one inn, not far from here. If you would care to join me?'

Stepping out into the darkness of the street, blinded by the change from the gas jet inside, Rantor stumbled and grasped at the wall for support.

'Damned torches. Always let you down when you need them! Hawk: your next job ought to be to find a way to make that lightning generator of yours provide a steady glow. Then we could –' He turned at a sound behind them, hand moving to his sword. 'Hold! Behind me, Hawk!'

Idiot! Of course those torches hadn't burned out yet, in this quarter of the dock patrolled by the Duke's men. Somebody was out there – somebody with eyes well adapted to the dark.

He drew the sword, edging backwards as he became aware of three – no, four – shadowy figures confronting him.

'In the Duke's name! I am the Navigator, Rantor. Anyone who harms me, or my companion, will answer to Lord Kyper.'

Surely nobody could be so foolish? Rantor himself represented the Duke's most valued possession. No rival lord would harm or kidnap the Navigator; several might like to, but that would give the Duke his excuse to crush the opponent foolhardy enough to take such action, picking off his adversaries one by one, before they could organize against him. All the lesser lords would support the Duke in any action he took in defence of the Navigator. Without navigation the Archipelago would cease to be civilized.

The figures moved, two straight for him, one to either side. Professionals. No chance, four against one, but they'd know they'd been in a fight. The sword flicked out, met another blade, parried. And swung to the side, striking at the second swordsman. Rantor felt the jar as it stabbed through flesh and jolted along bone. But before he could withdraw to strike again, two of the hooded figures held him in their grasp. The fourth had the terrified Hawk, who had taken no part in the action, at sword point.

Only now did one of his two captors speak, as the other bound Rantor's hands.

'My apologies, Navigator. We intend you no harm, but it seems expedient to borrow you for a while. It is your companion whose services we seek, and whose activities are of interest to our Lord.'

The second man turned his attention to his wounded companion who was leaning against the wall, holding his cloak against his side. They spoke briefly, then the wounded man moved off slowly, into the night, staying close by the wall. Their remaining captors pushed Rantor and Hawk back towards the workshop entrance, swords prominently displayed. In the doorway, a flash of reflected light showed where the guards, belatedly aroused by the scuffle, waited.

The same man, clearly the leader of the band, spoke up again.

'Guard! We have your Navigator, the esteemed Rantor, as you see. Duke Kyper would surely wish no harm to befall such a valuable servant! Give us access for a few minutes, and he will be released unharmed.'

The Navigator fumed inwardly. It would work, he knew. No soldier would risk the Duke's wrath by allowing Rantor to be harmed. Whatever their orders concerning the Hawk and his toys, the guards would only move against the kidnappers if there was no risk to Rantor. Not for the first time, he cursed his privileged position.

Inside, disarmed, bound and with cold steel to his throat, he could only watch, helplessly, as the first raider examined the impressive collection of apparatus, Hawk's lightning generator, at the near end of the gallery.

Under the threat of drawn weapons, there was silence in the chamber as the intruders went about their work. Outside, a creak of harness and a snuffle of horses indicated the arrival of more raiders, with transport. They intended, Rantor realized, to take the generator with them. Nothing could be done, unless the guards were willing to risk his life. For a moment he thought of flinging himself on a sword. If he were dead, the guards would have to act. But it was true – he was worth more than Hawk and his apparatus, quite apart from his reluctance to end his own life. But perhaps there was a way.

He flung up his arms, bound as they were, crying 'Hawk!' At that movement, the knife of his captor pressed more closely against his throat, drawing a red line of blood. 'Do as they command.' Emphasizing his words he dropped his arms back downward, clumsily but consciously echoing Hawk's earlier signal to his men. The pressure at his throat eased.

'Or you will never see another *dawn*. Do you understand? Take your machine, and use it as they command. This Navigator is indeed worth more to our Lord than you and all your toys. Is everything still in place?'

The bright, darting look of an intelligent bird was back in Hawk's eyes. As Rantor had hoped, he turned and walked back towards the generator, and made a show of inspecting it closely.

'Yes, Navigator, everything is here. All in working order.'

'Then let us go.' The chief raider spoke abruptly. Two other cloaked and hooded men had entered the room. He gestured at the generator, and at Hawk. 'Take everything, and him. The brave Navigator,' he raised his voice to the guards lined against the wall opposite, 'stays with us for a while. If no one follows, he will be released. Otherwise, your Duke can seek another to guide his ships.'

THREE

It was still dark when Elyse woke. Another useful skill she had learned during her time as a probationer – the ability to wake when she wanted, at the time she had repeated to herself, in her head, as she was going to sleep. The dream had been more vivid, though, than it had been for many days – indeed, since she had started to learn how to work with the woodsmoke. But then, she had had no opportunity to work properly with the smoke for two days, what with the preparation for her Testing and the Test itself. And there was Karyn's story of her voyage here, to the Halls. Perhaps that explained the vividness of Elyse's dream of a great ship. Though no ship she had ever seen, and certainly not the one which had carried Karyn from the Eastern Settlements, had ever been so large as the one she dreamed about.

But there was no time to wonder at the meaning of the dream, if it had any meaning at all. Quietly, Elyse slipped out of bed. She was already fully dressed, except for her boots and jacket. In the short tunic and trousers, with her hair pushed under a cap and with the loose jacket around her shoulders she would almost certainly be mistaken for a young man, at least in the gloom of the poorly lit streets outside. Most of the clothing Karyn had brought to her the previous day could be left behind; just a few possessions were stored away in the pack that she swung on to her back, adjusting the shoulder straps so that it fitted snugly, leaving her hands free. Far more important than the clothing were the tinder-box and flint, securely wrapped inside the pack, that she was starting to think of as the tools of her Talent. Now, all she had to do was get out of here, without disturbing the guard, and get far enough away to be safe from any pursuit organized by the Sisters before it became light and the waking bell sounded.

The guard – or at least, a guard; she assumed the other one had been relieved by now – was still outside her door, preventing any contact with the community in the Halls. But the window, which opened on to a small space between the quarters and the fence, was unguarded. This wasn't, after all, a prison. She was simply being treated like any visitor to the Halls, kept at arm's length except for official business. It was unthinkable that anyone who had been under the authority of the Sisters for so long would dream of doing anything except what she was told. And here she was, unthinkably, climbing the fence and dropping down on the other side, into the night-time darkness.

To her left, she could make out the loom of the tower by the gate. The track from there wound gently downhill to the township of Seahaven, a scattered community covering both banks of the Little River. Now, in high summer, the air was warm and dry, even this late at night. In winter, when the land cooled, cloud would often come spilling down from the White Mountains at night, bringing with it soft rain and mists. In the Halls, this passage of the seasons had passed almost unnoticed; but as she moved just a few paces away from the fence, and felt the stirring of the soft summer breeze, memories of her earlier life came flooding back. Yes, there was more to life than the Halls. And she would enjoy that life, and keep her Talent, as long as she possibly could.

The slim figure moved quietly away, downhill, but

keeping clear of the track from the Halls to Seahaven. That would be the first place where they would search for her. She was heading a little to the east, as well as downhill, away from the river and the town. What she needed was a fishing village, a small community where there might be someone willing to ferry her past the mouth of the Great River, and on to the Eastern Settlements. There was no way to cross the Great River without a boat, and she had nothing material to offer in payment for such a journey. But *perhaps* she had something of value to such a fishing community. The idea had been growing inside her almost from the moment she had made her decision to leave, fed by her careful questioning of Karyn and her own memories of the boats she had seen, but never travelled in, as a girl. All the real boats that she knew, big or small, had the same kind of square sail, mounted on a mast in the centre of the vessel. But the boats of her dreams, especially *the* ship, were different. And she was beginning to think she knew why.

First, she needed shelter during the day. One of the patches of woodland behind the coast would be ideal. Then, she needed to make a fire; but that could wait until nightfall. And tomorrow . . .

※　　※　　※

'Oh yes Lord, I'm certain enough.' The Navigator, unable to contain himself, strode impatiently to and fro across the large room, slapping his thigh with the gloves he carried in his right hand. He was dangerously close to insubordination, but the Duke had to permit him to act. He had played the coward intentionally, planning to rescue Hawk and his lightning machine and to strike a blow for the ruler of the Three Islands. If Duke Kyper's caution prevented him from moving, the story of his desertion of a servant in his charge would ring around the fleets of the world.

He stopped pacing, and faced the Duke squarely across the table, hands resting flat on the surface. 'They were Ballastre's men. I know their ship, and I can find the Hawk. He will voice a public protest and you will be free to slap Ballastre down. No one will interfere. Not Falco, nor Langan. You will have proven just cause.'

'And if you fail to find Hawk, but Ballastre finds you adventuring in his domain, then he will have just cause against me. Falco and Langan will side with him; others too, perhaps, while the lesser islands hold back.'

'But if you take no action, sire? This time, you have lost little. The machine is probably worthless; Hawk is a fool – you said so. But if word gets out that a raider from a Ballastre ship can take his pick of the property of Lord Kyper, in the middle of his own shipyard?'

The Duke looked steadily at his Navigator.

'You are so sure, then, that Hawk and his toys are worthless?'

Against that steely gaze, Rantor wilted. 'Lord, I . . .'

'And you would take such risks, solely for the honour of the Three Islands, and yourself?'

There was nothing more to say. Rantor felt a glow of triumph. The Duke might banter, but he was going to agree!

'How many men do you need?'

'Five double hands at most. The new ship, the *Far Trader*; and those two assistants Hawk was training.'

'And your plan?'

He shook his head. 'Forgive me, Lord. I fear that there are spies in our midst. How else could those raiders have known where and when to strike? But have faith, and in a fiveday, perhaps two, I shall return Hawk to you and give you just cause to strike at Ballastre. After that, no island will dare to cross you.'

The *Far Trader* slid slowly towards the beach, sails furled, under muffled oars only. At this time, just before dawn, the breeze was off the land. It would stay that way for some time after the sun began to glow, ideal for their escape. After six days, cruising slowly along these shores in the dark, and further out to sea in the early part of the day, the Navigator had a clear idea of the position of the Hawk. The hours spent closeted below decks seemed to have paid off, but his men knew only that he had the information required. The rumour below decks was that he had a spy in the enemy camp. He had encouraged the rumour, and his obvious confidence had encouraged the faith in both the rumour and himself.

Ballastre had, if Rantor was correct, chosen a good place for his captive to work. The isolated watch-tower was far enough from the town that any untoward events would cause no damage – Rantor remembered some of the mishaps in the early days of the gas lighting experiments and approved of such caution. The tower was also far from the harbour, up a steep path. No attack from that direction could possibly take its garrison by surprise. It was, however, vulnerable from another direction. A small landing party, in the bay around the headland, could approach the tower from the rear – if, that is, any such raiding party had reason to suspect the activities now going on there. Ballastre had taken pains to ensure that no hint of those activities had leaked out. But he was in for a surprise.

'This will do.' Rantor spoke quietly, but without whispering. The Captain nodded, and gave the necessary order in an equally matter-of-fact voice. The chain of command was clear, and established by long practice. The Navigator decided what to do, where to go, and when. The Captain decided how to do it, and ran the ship. If a Navigator asked the impossible, or demanded a course that would lead his ship into danger, a captain might refuse and argue his case later with the Duke. But this was almost unheard of. Navigators didn't get to be Navigators by taking unnecessary risks.

A single anchor at the stern held the ship with the bows pointing seaward in the light breeze. With the oars shipped, two boats were lowered into the water.

'Pull!' A single word sent the laden boats scudding into land. With two men left to guard them, Rantor had just fifteen at his back as he led the way up the slope to the tower. They stopped in the cover of a small copse, perhaps a hundred paces from the target. The ground between was scrubby. Sloppy work, thought Rantor, as he checked out a possible way forward. At a gesture two bowmen and two others with ropes coiled over their shoulders stepped forward. Wordlessly, Rantor pointed a way forward, from cover to cover. Then he pointed up to the top of the tower, ten span above their heads. The four nodded and moved swiftly forward, lost in the darkness and the bushes.

The sound of the two grappling-hooks biting into the top

of the tower was swiftly followed by the twang of two bows and a stifled cry – as, if all had gone to plan, the sentries drawn by the noise of the grapples had been picked off from the roof.

Waving his men on, Rantor ran forward and swiftly began to ascend one of the ropes.

✳   ✳   ✳

It was a tired, dirty, hungry and desperately thirsty Elyse that stumbled into the village the next morning. But a fire burned within her. The smoke had bent to her will as never before, bringing her pictures of the great ship at sea, tearing through the waves. She could still picture the way it moved, the line of the sails and the rigging. In her trance she had almost imagined that she could feel the wind that it cut through, and hear the chuckle of the water foaming under its prow. But none of that mattered. What mattered was that she was sure she was right. That this was a real ship, somewhere, moving through a real ocean, with the aid of a real wind, in whatever strange world of islands where it belonged. And if the ship were real, then her idea would work.

The village consisted of a cluster of log cabins, dotted around a central open area, some distance from the shore. Thin wisps of smoke rose from the holes in one or two of the roofs; hens scratched about in the dust. Further over, right on the shoreline itself, there were three cruder huts, festooned with netting, ropes, floats and other equipment. Several men were working amongst the paraphernalia. Elyse skirted the houses and the huts, heading at an angle across the beach to her objective.

At the water's edge, she leaned for a while on a wooden breakwater, looking intently at the line of small boats drawn up on the beach. Most were upside down on the sand, their round, shallow bottoms scoured by the many times they had been hauled up out of the water, or pushed back down into it. Two boats, at the water's edge, were upright, their solitary masts stepped in place. Elyse smiled. One of the two had its single sail already fixed to the – what was it called? The boom? – lying squarely across the little vessel, ready for hoisting.

That one. Whoever owned that boat wasn't a man for wasting time. He'd probably be a leader in this small community. Halls training gave her confidence in her decision. She stepped out, determinedly but licking her dry lips, for the boat that was most nearly ready for sea, and the two men – no, one man and a young boy – that were working on it.

The man was tall, bearded, with a deep tan. He was doing something incomprehensible with fishing nets and bits of line, and didn't deign to look up at her approach, although the youth stopped working and stared at her openly.

'An' what 'ave we 'ere, then?'

Even while he spoke, the hands still picked over the netting, and he kept his eyes on his work.

'If you please ...' Elyse stopped, her hoarse voice scarcely more than a whisper.

The fisherman looked up, took in her unkempt appearance, the smears of charcoal on her face and hands.

'Fetch some water, Jak.'

The boy turned and ran across the beach to the nearest hut, where a small group of men were gathering, staring at the new arrival.

'Sit down, lad. No hurry. Have you come far?'

She nodded. The further he thought she'd come, the better – and he'd called her 'lad'. She sat on the rough wooden box that he indicated, hunched forward to keep the folds of the jacket as loose as possible around her body.

'Up river?'

She nodded again, just as Jak returned with a wooden beaker of water. Smiling her thanks, she took it from him and drank deeply, wiping her mouth with the back of a hand, and smearing more dust and charcoal across it in the process. The less clear a view this sharp-eyed sailor had of her face the better.

'Thank you.' She returned the beaker to the boy. The fisherman bent to his work again. He seemed happy to take the lead in their conversation, and she was happy to let him. Training, again: in negotiations, let the other party talk as much as possible, and learn anything you could from their remarks. She had already learned that the community here wasn't too surprised to be visited by a dishevelled stranger from up river, and simply by keeping quiet she had ended up with the beginnings of a plausible background, better than any story she might have concocted.

'We don't see many folks from up river down this way. What brings you here?'

'I'm going to the Eastern Settlements. To visit relations. Gregor, the blacksmith.'

The man used his teeth to help him tie a knot, then laid the netting down, studying her again.

'Aye. That'll be the drought, no doubt. Not much meat on your bones, but your folks can manage better, for sure, with one less mouth to feed.'

'The drought?'

He smiled, and reached over to pat her on the leg.

'We may not see many visitors from up river, but news travels faster than any man. An' sure, the drought's bad enough across the whole land. I hope your cousin the blacksmith has food enough for you, young – now, did I not catch your name?'

'Alyn.'

'And I'm Nathan.' He held out a hand, which she shook as firmly as she could manage. 'And Jak you know, and this,' he patted the side of the boat, 'is *Merry*, though not as merry as we'd all be if the fish were runnin' stronger.' And he laughed loudly at the little joke, while she smiled uncertainly, and wondered what turn this conversation was going to take. She temporized, plausibly, she hoped.

'There's plenty of food in the Settlements. No drought on the banks of the Great River.'

He nodded. 'Reckon not.' There was a pause, while the big man weighed things up.

'So you're Alyn, from up river, on your way to visit your cousin Gregor, the blacksmith, in the Eastern Settlements.'

She nodded again.

'You won't get there without a boat.'

Ah! That was what he had been working towards.

'That's why I'm here.'

'And why pick on Nathan, and the *Merry*? There's good sailors over there,' he nodded towards the huts, 'that you passed by without so much as a good day. Not, though, that any one of 'em wouldn't acknowledge who was the best sailor around here. But who told you?'

'You told me yourself.' He looked surprised, but waited for her to continue. 'Which boat is ready for sea? Who has already finished preparing his nets, while the others gossip like old women?'

The great roar of laughter came again, as he slapped her on the back. 'You've got sharp eyes, lad. An' a clear mind, to be sure. Maybe you won't do so bad in the Settlements, an' all.'

He turned to look at the group of men by the huts, nodding in acknowledgement of their half-waves. It was

47

clear that they did hold him in some regard, and would not disturb his interrogation of the stranger. Once again, he was quiet, mulling things over. Then he turned to look out to sea, speaking quietly, almost to himself.

'Two days, with a fair wind. An' two days back again. A man can catch a lot of fish in four days, even if they're runnin' slow.'

'I can't pay.'

'Reckon not. Reckon those as can pay might be over in Seahaven.'

'But I've got something ... I've got an idea ... that is, I think I know a way ...' It sounded so silly, now that she came to put it into words. A tough, experienced sailor like this, with many summers behind him. How could she possibly persuade him that she knew more about sailing than he did? But there was no point in dithering. Training again: be confident, and however much you doubt your own ability, leave no room for others to doubt. He wasn't looking out to sea any more. She felt his eyes burning into the top of her lowered head.

She raised her head, looked him straight in the eye.

'I *do* know a way to make your boat sail better.'

'Better?'

'Differently. Against the wind.'

'Now, that *would* be a neat trick.' The roaring laugh came again. 'Worth four days' fishin', that's for sure. And how come you know such a trick, up river, where there's no call for any sailin' at all?'

This was it. The point of no return. She'd either get a hearing, at least, or be on her way back to the Sisters this very day.

'Halls Knowledge.'

'Halls Knowledge?' He leaned towards her, suddenly serious, reached an instant decision. 'Jak, lad. You run along now. Tell your mother we've a guest.' He stood up, looked about him as Jak scampered off, nodded at the group of fishermen by the hut. Turning, he gazed out to sea, shook his head. 'I don't like the look of the weather, anyway.' Puzzled, Elyse followed his gaze, out across the blue sea, where birds were wheeling about under a few puffy clouds. Nathan stretched his arms above his head and turned back to her, folding them across his chest. 'No fishin' today.' He stood, silent for a moment, looking down at where she still sat on the wooden box. 'What do you know of the witches, lad?'

Witches! For a moment, Elyse was on the brink of an angry retort. The Sisters weren't witches! But the expression had been common enough when she was a child, even if she hadn't heard it these past four summers, and, she told herself, it showed a pleasing lack of reverence, given her present circumstances.

'I have a sister. A probationer in the Halls. And my mother,' improvising wildly, Elyse began to elaborate her story, 'she was once a probationer, too.'

'So you really do have Halls Knowledge, eh lad? A present from your mother, to pay your way to the East . . . well, I've heard stranger tales. And there's witches' blood in your body.' She felt a blush rising to her cheeks, and hung her head, keeping quiet. 'Well, better you told this to Nathan than to some I could name. And better we say no more about it, as long as you're my guest. We pay our tithes to the Halls, and we follow the Law, poor though we be. But times are hard, and there's many as think the witches could share that hardship, not keep on increasing the tithes with every season that passes. Halls Knowledge to help with the fishin', now, that would be only our fair due, no mistake. But will this Knowledge of yours help me to catch fish?'

She stood. 'It will make your boat sail against the wind. If that will help you to catch fish, then it will help you to catch fish.'

'Witchcraft. But if it works, good payment for a four-day voyage. Come.' And, without waiting for her to respond, he was striding off across the sand, in the direction that young Jak had run before.

By nightfall, she was in despair. Everyone had been kind to her. She was well-fed, no longer thirsty, and reasonably clean. But Nathan refused to accept her 'Knowledge'. She had drawn in the sand with sticks, and made herself hoarse again trying to explain the importance of the flat, triangular sail attached to a long boom sticking out *forwards* from the bow of the ship. But he had simply shaken his head, repeating in his firm way that such a *sideways* sail could not possibly make a boat move against the wind, and would only succeed in getting it blown sideways through the water.

It didn't help that she was so obviously ignorant of the sailor's language, and didn't know the names of any of the things she was trying to describe to him. What, he asked reasonably, was to stop the boat from sliding sideways through the water? He refused even to entertain the idea of wasting time building such a rig for the *Merry*. And he made it plain that while he would never turn a guest from his door, there was no prospect of a voyage to the Eastern Settlements.

It was also plain that the guest, being not much more than a lad, would be expected to share young Jak's bed. Reasonable enough – even generous – but offering little prospect of maintaining the fiction of 'Alyn'. Which was the clinching factor that had brought her back out into the woods, after dinner, striking sparks into the tinder, catching a small flame and transferring it to the prepared pile of dry leaves and twigs, with a double handful of green leaves alongside.

The Talent couldn't fail her now. There must be more to the trick of sailing against the wind than she had seen with her untutored eye, but which now, in the light of Nathan's insight, would be clear to her. She could *feel* the power within herself, and knew that even a small fire would suffice. She settled with her back against a tree, legs folded in front of her, and threw the green stuff on to the flames. Resting her hands in her lap, she gazed into the smoke, watching it take shape.

It was as if she were there, on the deck of the great ship, as it heeled in the wind. Men ran to haul on ropes, the water gurgled over the side. There were birds, flying above the banked clouds of the sails. The vision was more real than it had ever been, and had come so quickly; her burning need had carried her swiftly into the trance state. But still, she knew that she was merely a spectator, and that this was not the vision she needed. The ship leaned to the right – to *starboard*, as Nathan called it – and, looking that way, she could see another vessel, long and slender, carrying a single mast with one square sail, being propelled by the rhythmic thrust of the dozen or more oars that lined each side. The wind was blowing across the other boat, and its sail was canted to catch the breeze, boosting its speed. But the main driving force came from the oars, pushing it forwards. The effect of the sail was more to move the boat sideways than ahead. It was sliding sideways through the water, just as Nathan had said the *Merry* would, if he fitted her out with 'Alyn's' strange rig. But there were no rows of oarsmen in the *Merry* to keep the boat moving forward as well as sideways, creeping crabwise across the water.

In spite of the combination of oars and sail on the other vessel, it was clear that the ship would pass well in front of it, heading at an angle into the wind. Elyse was sure she could hear laughter, far off, and the distant sound of bare feet on planking as the men moved about the deck. But the noises were as indistinct and dreamlike as her first smoke visions of the ship had been. They meant nothing. But why could the ship outsail the rowers?

Suddenly, the vision shifted. She was on the prow of the rowing-boat – the *galley*. The term came unbidden into her mind, together with the realization that she was seeing things, had *always* been seeing things in her dreams, through the eyes of another person. She was not a disembodied observer, but saw *only* what somebody, somewhere, really saw. And this particular somebody was half angry, half impressed as he (?) watched the ship pass on its way, crossing in front of the galley, heeling so far that the outline of the keel could be seen through the clear water before it forged away, with a few waves and a derisory shout from the men on the after deck.

She woke with a start, tongue glued to the roof of her mouth, back aching from the pressure of the tree trunk, legs stiff and cramped. The fire had completely burned out. Where was she? For an instant, the ground seemed strangely still, to senses long accustomed to the heave of a deck beneath her feet. She shook her head. What was she thinking? She had *never* felt the heave of a deck beneath her feet! But as she stood, a combination of the cramp in her legs and the sudden dizziness of unstable sea legs made her stagger, clutch at the nearest tree for support.

The 'tree' clutched her back.

'Steady, lad.'

Nathan!

'Strange behaviour, even for one with witches' blood in him. Or maybe not so strange. Can you walk?'

She nodded, before realizing that she was as invisible to him as he was to her.

'Yes.' She shrugged off the helping hand. 'I'm fine.' The gumminess was dissolving out of her mouth. 'And I know what else we need to make your boat sail against the wind.'

'Aye. No doubt your mother told you. Or the firelight.'

He knew!

'Best be getting back. You'll need some sleep. I'll send Jak to lie by the boat; it's a fine enough night. You can have his bed, all to yourself. People with witches' blood need a bit of privacy, I reckon.'

They set off through the gloom together, Elyse's mind in turmoil. He knew, and he wasn't going to send her back. Did he defy the Halls through his hope to gain from her Knowledge? Or out of bitterness at the tithes imposed on his village? She wouldn't ask, and she didn't care. But she would repay the kindness in full. The sideways sail, as Nathan had realized, was no good on its own. You had to stop the boat drifting sideways through the water. And what stopped it sliding sideways was the wood sticking down beneath it – the *keel*. She shook her head, It seemed to be full of strange new words. *Keel. Galley. Heel.* For a moment, she felt the ship move beneath her feet, staggered. Nathan caught her arm, steadied her; this time, she didn't shrug the grip away.

Of course, you couldn't just stick a lump of wood on the bottom of the *Merry*. But something fastened to the side, perhaps, that you could raise up when the boat came into shore, lower when you were out at sea. Or something fastened to both sides; surely that would be twice as good? And the *Merry* would be the first boat in all the Land to sail against the wind, and it would carry her beyond the Great River, to the Eastern Settlements.

Would he really do it, this tough, practical fisherman, who had been so reluctant to follow her advice today? Would he believe that two boards fixed to the sides of his boat would make all the difference? Dreamily, half sleepwalking, she knew that he would. Now that he knew that she was a 'witch' herself, now that he had seen that she had a Talent. Hearsay from a stray youth might be ignored; the visions of a Sister were always taken seriously. It was almost as clear in her mind as one of the smoke visions themselves. If a respectable fisherman like Nathan, so close to the Halls, was willing to defy the Sisters, in his own quiet way, then Karyn's brother Gregor, far away in the east, would surely welcome her and find her a home. Even with a useless Talent, she would be able to take the role of a wise woman, settling disputes with the aid of her Halls training, perhaps doing a little healing.

But was her Talent so useless? The stray thought roused her briefly from her sleepwalking. A Talent that could teach fishermen new tricks, and better ways to sail? Her heart beat faster at the thought. She had found a way to use her Talent after all! The Sisters were wrong, and if she had obeyed them, the Talent would have been lost for ever. There could have been no clearer sign that she had taken the right path. Perhaps there were new tricks her visions could show her to impress even a blacksmith with her knowledge!

She smiled to herself in the dark, stumbling slightly and leaning against Nathan for support. She was *so* tired. Praise be, she didn't have to pretend, at least to him; and double praise that she had a bed all to herself to look forward to, and all the sleep she could use, in the little house that they were approaching. Sleep, with or without dreaming, was all she needed just now.

※　　※　　※

The action was over in minutes. It was still dark as the party returned to the boats, carrying one dead, two wounded, and the large glass jars which Hawk insisted they could not leave without. The burdens slowed them down more than Rantor expected; in addition, someone had been left at the tower with their wits about them, and sufficiently unscathed to mount the stairs of the tower. The boats were still pulling hard for the *Far Trader* when an orange glow appeared on the headland. First a mere flicker of flame, but soon burgeoning into a leaping pillar of light. Cursing, the Navigator exhorted the already straining men at the oars to pull harder. Even as they came alongside the ship, however, he knew that Ballastre's vessels in the harbour round the headland would already be bustling with life and preparing for action. It would be nip and tuck. Just let *Far Trader* get to seaward of Ballastre's ships, and he was sure the captain would show them a clean pair of heels. But if they were cut off . . .

'Abandon the boats!' Captain Bryon was clearly aware of the need for haste. 'Cut the cable. Get those men on to the deck. And all sail.' This with a glance back towards the dark land behind him, not so much to see the land as to feel the dying breeze on his cheek, gauging how much life there was left in it. Just let them get to seaward of the fleet, and with the sun bringing the sea breeze on to the land nobody would ever catch the *Far Trader*. Scarcely twenty leagues away, through the doldrums, the welcoming breeze on to the land would usher them swiftly home to the Three Islands.

'Careful there!' Hawk's cry came as a stumbling seaman

threatened to drop one of his jars. 'Put it here, on the deck. Navigator,' he turned, 'it was brilliantly done. I take it the sensor worked?' They clasped hands, sharing their delight in the brief lull while the captain prepared the ship for action.

'Beautifully. Oh,' a dismissive wave, 'I don't say we didn't have some troubles. But your assistants are well trained. Every dawn, as we patrolled, they found your signal. The direction-finding is poor, but with three successive bearings, why, even the most unlikely 'prentice Navigator could have pinned you down to the headland – and there is only one place on the headland where you could have been. My only concern was that you would misunderstand my intentions, or be unable to persuade your temporary master to allow you to experiment.'

Hawk laughed. 'No fear of that. They'd have had me at work night and day, once I let on that I was developing a technique to turn rock into metal. Duke Ballastre is a greedy man. But I persuaded him that my method depended on striking a resonance with the newborn sun – and also, of course, that it required some separation from the centre of the town. I had those soldiers of his fair jumping every time I shouted "frog". But tell me,' his voice changed as he looked about, 'we are still in danger, are we not?'

Rantor, also suddenly grave, looked about the darkened ship, where only a few faint lights relieved the gloom. The headland must be there – his sense of direction seldom failed him, even in the pitch of night – sure enough, just beyond he caught a quick flash of light, then a second. He nodded at his companion.

'Grave danger, friend. On the open sea, no ship could find us, or board, at night. But here, with only one clear channel, they can feel their way out,' he nodded, forward to where a stocky sailor was coiling a long line, attached to a stone, ready to throw it over the side to gauge the depth of water, 'and cut us off. A little longer, half a candle or less, and we might have been clear. As it is . . .' He shrugged.

'Perhaps I can help. Your Captain – is he a good man? Will he follow my advice?'

'Bryon? We've often sailed together. If I give the word, he would sail into the maelstrom itself. But if you have a plan, be quick about it, for time is short indeed.'

Three ships, their riding lights clear, blocked the channel ahead of the *Far Trader*. Ahead, tantalizingly close, lay the open sea, and freedom.

Backing her oars, the *Far Trader* slowed almost to a halt, but continued to drift down on the ships. At the word of command, she could surge forward – to certain destruction, or if the other ships allowed her, to an instant escape. The catapults were wound and armed, but they were inaccurate weapons at best in broad daylight. Naval engagements were settled by boarding and hand-to-hand fighting. Besides, it was one against three.

'Yield! Yield or suffer the consequences!' Astonishingly, the cry came from Captain Bryon, at the bow of the ship.

There was a brief silence. Were they stunned by his audacity? Or simply sorting out seniority among the gaggle of seamen, soldiers and civil administrators aboard the craft? Bryon pressed home his slender, momentary advantage.

'We have the Hawk. And his weapon. Yield, or we will use it.'

At last, the reply came. But it lacked the confident tone of Bryon.

'There is no weapon. We have the advantage and you must yield to us. We have no reason to fear you.'

The Hawk, busy at the bows of the *Far Trader* with his two assistants and a mess of equipment, centred around those glass jars he treasured so much, nodded to the Captain. With the slow forward way still on her, the *Far Trader* was scarcely a stone's throw from the ships blocking the path. The Navigator, in the waist of the ship, murmured a quick 'Ready' to the oarsmen. At the bow, Bryon raised his voice again.

'We will give you one chance. Our Hawk commands the lightning. One time, and one time only, he will demonstrate his power. Then you must yield, and follow us to the Three Islands. Or be struck down where you lie.'

He raised his right hand. 'Be warned, you doubters!' He let it fall. There was a brilliant flash from the bows, a shaft of lightning fully a span in length, arcing and wriggling across the bows, almost touching the nearest Ballastre vessel. A strange pungent smell, a smell of lightning, drifted back. Cries of alarm came from the ships ahead, as their oarsmen, unbidden, began to back water. A gap appeared.

'Now!' cried the Navigator, and the disciplined oarsmen of the *Far Trader* laid to their task. The ship shot for the gap, and was through in two strokes. Three, and there was clear water behind her; four, five and she was away, in the dying sea breeze, heading for the open ocean. With the oarsmen given strength by the thrill of their success, and their opponents thrown into disarray, however temporarily, their safety was assured.

Forgetting his dignity, the Navigator ran forward to where the Hawk glumly surveyed the wreckage of the equipment. Oblivious to the congratulations being showered upon him, he looked up only at Rantor's hail.

'Well done. Oh, well done, indeed. This story will be told in all the ports on the Archipelago! The night the Hawk brought down the lightning!'

'Aye, but at what cost?' Hawk indicated the wreckage of the equipment, metal melted into fantastic shapes. The small sphere from the sensor, unrecognizably distorted; glass jars broken.

At Hawk's feet, a half-sphere of metal, about the size of a cupped fist, rocked slightly with the motion of the ship. It was part of one of the larger spheres, come apart around its seam. He picked it up, holding it in the palm of one hand. At the bottom of the hemisphere, a small puddle of water had collected from the spray; following the natural tendency of things to seek the lowest point, it sloshed to and fro and as Hawk swayed with the roll of the ship. He inverted the hemisphere, and the water fell out on to the deck. Miserably, he offered the useless object to Rantor.

'This is ruined, and the rest has been left behind. Many seasons of work.'

'But you have your life, Hawk, and your liberty. Never fear for these trifles. Ballastre is disgraced, by your testimony, and our Lord Kyper will be generous in gratitude. This ship will be fitted out with all that you require, and together we will sail beyond the Archipelago, sure of finding our way home. What sights we shall see, Hawk, if your philosophizing is correct, and what riches we shall bring back!'

His enthusiastic excitement roused Hawk from his gloom. 'You really think so? It isn't an unmitigated disaster after all?'

'Oh no, my friend. At last I know what my life has been leading up to and where I am going. You have given me a new sense of direction and I thank you for it.'

As if to emphasize his words, the sun high over their heads lit up in its usual manner. It was dawn; the dawn of a new era for the Navigators of the Archipelago.

Patterns of impulses raced at the speed of light through an alien mind, collating, observing, interpreting. Especially observing; that had been the task of the mind since time immemorial. Responding to an ancient imperative, the observer watched and waited, patient as only inorganic intelligence could be, for the signs it had been programmed to detect.

The disturbances caused by the lightning generator had briefly held its attention. Weak, erratic and probably natural disturbances in the electromagnetic spectrum, coming from the region of a small group of islands in the southern hemisphere. They contained no information, though, and they stopped after a few cycles of light and dark. They were not the signs of intelligence that the observer was programmed to recognize. It felt no disappointment. This was far from being the first time that some temporary change in environmental conditions had suggested, erroneously, that the long wait was over, and besides the observer was not programmed for emotions. The incident was noted for comparison and cross-correlation with future disturbances. The observer went about its business quietly, calmly, as it had done for millennia past.

FOUR

Leaning on the rail, he watched Hawk trying to set fire to the ship, while Captain Bryon ostentatiously kept out of the way below decks, making it clear that he had nothing to do with this madness. The Navigator asked himself, not for the first time, just how he had arrived in this insane position. Fire on board a ship at sea! To think he had lived to see this. Rantor glanced up at the almost cloudless sky, with the sun, as always, at the zenith. In the habitual gesture that had become automatic, he mopped at his forehead and the back of his neck with a large red kerchief. He shifted position slightly, to take benefit from the modest amount of shade offered by the sail, barely drawing in the light wind, and leaned forward again to watch the antics going on in the waist of the ship.

There were enough volunteers ready to participate in any crazy task that the Hawk might set them – you had to be half crazy in any case to volunteer for this voyage into the un-known, sailing far beyond sight of land. Students, half of them, granted leave of absence by the priests who ran the college, back in the Archipelago. And you could be sure that anyone the priests granted leave of absence to was someone they were glad to have out of their hair. A sprinkling of good sailors, of course – men who would follow their Captain any-where.

As for Captain Bryon himself, he was here because he trusted the Navigator, the man in charge of this expedition. But why was Rantor here? He asked himself the same question every day, and had yet to find a satisfactory answer. The *un*satisfactory answer was that he was here because he had faith in what most people thought of as the strangest man ever to live on the Islands (a thought usually qualified by the comment that, after all, he *was* an outsider, from some remote atoll far across the Archipelago).

A couple of nervous sailors were tending a brazier of hot charcoal, under the supervision of that little man, naked to the waist and smeared with soot until he looked like a devil. What other men regarded as mundane, the Hawk's far-seeing eyes found strange; what he seemed to think was normal, most men found incomprehensible. And yet, enough of his curious ideas had borne fruit to tempt the Navigator into following where Hawk pointed, ostensibly in the hope of finding wealth and fame, in reality because – well, because it felt good to do something out of the ordinary himself.

Only the Hawk could have persuaded the Navigator to allow a fire to be lit while the precious *Far Trader* was in the open sea, even under conditions as calm as this. Only under the direct orders of the Navigator would Captain Bryon, responsible for running the ship and for the safety of his crew, have allowed such insanity. In a wooden vessel, out of sight of land, with the sun beating down, fire was the sailors' greatest dread – but Hawk said it was important. The damnable thing was, Hawk needed calm conditions for his experimenting, and calm conditions meant that it was infernally hot, with sails and cordage ready to flare like tinder at the touch of a spark. In eight fivedays of voyaging, this was the worst possible time to be lighting fires.

Just what was important about the way sparks flew up into the air from a fire, Rantor could not comprehend. Everyone knew that sparks flew upward – that was why, unbidden, half a dozen crew members had manned the rigging, watching out for any errant specks of fire from the Hawk's activities, and snuffing them out before they could alight on the dry sails. Sparks, though, scarcely seemed to be good enough for Hawk.

Scraps of cloth, of various sizes, were consigned to the glowing brazier, and wafted up from it as they writhed and burned. There were even some sheets of precious paper, which the Hawk seemed particularly interested in, but which were the greatest cause of concern to the sailors. As the paper floated upwards it was still on fire, in the process of being consumed into charcoal wafers that drifted up and eventually out, under the watchful gaze of the crew, many span from the ship.

Watching the sparks rising above the brazier, Rantor caught sight of the sun, and shivered, in spite of the heat. Hawk's latest crazy notion could not possibly hold truth, could it? But if it were true, sparks were to blame. Sparks, of a different kind, were responsible for them being here, so far from home. The Hawk's strange signalling device, the morphic resonator, had faithfully reproduced its little flashes of artificial lightning every dawn, in response to the action of the large lightning generator installed in the topmost tower of the castle of Lord Kyper, at home in the Three Islands. Rantor remembered the demonstration of the morphic effect, back in the castle: how the banks of electric storage jars, discharging across a gap between two metal rods, had produced the lightning and the thunder, with an acrid smell, like that of Hell itself; and how, at the far end of the long gallery, the miniature replica of the lightning machine had produced its own feeble sparks in tune with the flash of lightning and crash of thunder, although it was untouched by any human operator. For all Hawk's fine talk of the scientific principles of morphic resonance – the law of similarities which required that like objects must behave in similar fashion, in tune with each other even when separated by great distances – it still seemed like magic, and not entirely white magic, to the Navigator. He remembered too well the tales from his childhood, in the village where, it was said, Grandma Holly could cure

64

an ague by applying a poultice to a clay figure of the sufferer, or (the whispers went) kill a goat with a pin stuck through a figurine. But, magic or not, Hawk's trick worked; and at heart Rantor was a practical man, not a religious one. If it worked, his creed said, then use it.

It was Hawk's genius that turned the resonator into a directional beacon. The metal shield, mounted on a track on the upper deck, a little wagon rolling in rails around a circle, pushed this way and that by a laughing gang of Hawk's most ardent 'prentices (who were, almost by definition, the most incompetent sailors on board). When the shield was in line between the resonator and the lightning generator, the generator could blast away for all it was worth, and not a spark would be seen in the resonator. But displace the shield to one side, and the sparks appeared. Metal blocked the resonant corpuscles. Why, even Hawk could not say (nor could he fathom the strange way in which, the further they got from the castle, the more it seemed that the sparks in the resonator were *strongest* when the metal shield was on the *far* side of the resonator from the lightning generator). The discovery had been an accident, and Hawk had lost interest in it once it had been made to work – and once he had failed to explain it. But its value had been obvious to the Navigator, well versed in his craft and in the mathematics of trigonometry.

With a tried and tested navigation beacon to point their way home, and a sound ship under them, the crew of the *Far Trader* were the first people to sail far out of sight of the Archipelago and yet expect to return home safely. They were following a course from which nobody had ever returned, and even the most ardent of Hawk's followers, Rantor guessed, probably gave thanks each morning that they had not fallen off the edge of the world in the night. As the days had added up, and then the fivedays in their turn, it had not escaped his notice that a little crowd of casual observers would gather just before the sun cast the nightglow aside, ready to check that there was still open sea ahead. Each day, the result had been the same. One moment, straining like the others to see beyond the bowsprit in the nightglow; the next, the reassuring return of the sun, blazing out from its accustomed position at the zenith and lighting the ocean ahead. Always, open ocean, as far as the eye could see. Although he would admit it to no man, Rantor himself felt a flow of relief each morning when the ritual was safely accomplished.

Sparks had brought them here – beyond, far beyond the point where unbelievers said the edge of the world must be. The priests who taught that the world was an infinite plane seemed to be vindicated with every day that passed. And yet, by bringing them here, sparks were responsible for Hawk's heretical new ideas, that cut away the foundations of a lifetime of belief from beneath the Navigator. Some nights before, in the cool of the after deck, Hawk had explained his vision to the Navigator.

'Well, Hawk.' The Navigator had been in a mellow mood, happy, as ever, to be at sea – in spite of his worries concerning the outcome of the mission. 'Two days since we had a spark out of that resonator of yours. And yet, I believe I might find my way back to the Three Islands after all.' He gestured to the misty nebulosity glowing low in the sky behind the ship. 'We may need your toy when we are closer to home, and the light fades. But by then, I have no doubt, you will come to our aid, eh?'

The Hawk was in a more reflective mood, unwilling to respond in kind to the bantering tone. 'You can use the glow as a beacon, Navigator. But I don't understand it. This far from land, all the torches in all the islands of the Archipelago could not produce a light bright enough for us to steer by. And that is no torchlight. It is too pale, and blue. If the air above the islands shines by night, why did we never notice, we who have spent all our lives in the Archipelago?'

'Hawk questions!' Rantor laughed. 'Why and how are no concerns of mine. Perhaps God sent the glow to guide wandering sailormen. All I care is that your sparks have brought us far enough out to sea for the lights in the sky to be made plain – both astern and,' he pointed, 'ahead. I'll never doubt you again, Hawk. The lights in the sky *are* other islands – other worlds – and *Far Trader* will live up to her name. We will all be rich, and famous, when we return to Lord Kyper's domain!'

'But why and how, my good Navigator, concern me greatly. How do the lights in the sky shine? And, most pressing in my mind at present, why are they above our heads? Always, we have to look up to the lights. Does that not make you wonder, with your training in geometry and navigation?'

Rantor frowned, his mood broken. 'The inner sphere? But it is a logical absurdity.'

'That rather depends on your point of view.'

The Hawk, it seemed, was getting around to the point that had been worrying him. He leaned forward, ticking items off on his fingers to emphasize the logic of his argument. Rantor noticed, with some amusement, that even Hawk now braced himself with legs wide apart, like a true sailorman, swaying gently with the roll of the ship as it glided over the sea under half sail in the light breeze. The wake behind seemed to glow with a life of its own, marking their arrow-straight course through the night. All was well with the ship, but Hawk's words removed some of the sense of well-being.

'We know that the sun is always at the zenith, viewed from anywhere in the Archipelago, or even, we see now, from outside. A line of sight to the sun is always perpendicular to the surface of the world. Parallel lines meet only at infinity, so the sun, we are taught, must be infinitely far away, and the world is an infinite flat plane. Unless –'

'Unless the world is really the inner surface of a sphere, with the sun at the centre. Yes, yes. But that is absurd. I mentioned that, back in Kyper's keep, only to *demonstrate* its absurdity – the law of the absurd alternative. If we live on the inner surface of a sphere, why doesn't all the water slop down to the bottom and drown us? If the sun isn't infinitely far away, why doesn't it fall down and burn us? Come, Hawk, you'll have to do better than that.'

'What is absurd, Navigator, depends, as I say, on your point of view. The priests who taught you your geometry are honest men, but they have only a limited view, confined to one Archipelago. Now we have travelled further – further than any man who has lived and returned to tell the tale. And we see behind us a glow, a glow that can *only* mark the Archipelago – though I admit we don't know how, or why – and that glow rises in the sky behind us as we advance. We see a glow ahead, that I will stake my life marks another Archipelago, dropping down the sky to meet us as we advance. And we see the sun, just as at home, vertically above our heads. We *must* be moving over the inner sphere. From our point of view, the law of the absurd alternative tells us that it is *impossible* for the world to be flat. And that means that the sun *is* only a finite distance above our heads. If I had a means to measure the distance we have travelled from the Archipelago, then all I would have to do is measure the angle to that light in the sky behind us and I could tell you just how far above us the sun sits – how far it is to the centre of the sphere.'

Instinctively, the Navigator, though scarcely a religious man, made the sign to ward off evil. 'And what keeps it there, floating above us while all other things fall to the surface of the world? What keeps an ocean of water poised like a wave above our heads, instead of flooding to the bottom of the sphere?'

The Hawk smiled. Rantor recognized the grin, and began to wonder what he was letting himself in for this time.

'Ah, Navigator. I have an idea about that. I thought – perhaps tomorrow if there is not too much wind – you might permit me to carry out a few simple tests.'

It had not, in fact, happened the next day. Strong winds, fair for their course, had blown them on for four days, while the night-time glow in the sky ahead, where Hawk had staked his life they would find another Archipelago, dropped down and dimmed into insignificance. Even under reduced sail, the *Far Trader* had ripped through the water, heeling to the wind until the lee rail dipped into each rolling wave as it lifted beneath them. Bryon had done well. Over the preceding fivedays, his crew of half-trained volunteers, still wet behind the ears when they had left the Three Islands, might not have become the best sailors in the Archipelago, but they were no longer fumbling incompetents.

Rantor remembered with pleasure the feel of the deck alive beneath his feet, and the spray stinging sharp against his cheek. The sailors had a saying that there was no such thing as bad weather – the only bad day for sailing was when there was no weather at all, in a flat calm. Give them wind, and a good ship, and they would voyage anywhere to find a profit for their Lord and a bonus for themselves. Another day at that pace, and they would be among the islands, if islands there were; Hawk had begged for permission to carry out his fire-raising before then, but neither Rantor nor Captain Bryon would relent until the wind dropped.

Now, though, Hawk had his chance, almost as if the wind had dropped in response to his entreaties. At least half the crew thought Hawk was a wizard anyway, and this happy coincidence (Rantor told himself he was sure it *was* a coincidence) would do his reputation no harm. The Navigator knew that it was worth giving the Hawk his head, within reason, and it was better for him to get this current madness out of his system before they arrived in a strange island, where Hawk's talent for observation could prove invaluable to the traders. There would be plenty for all to do, tomorrow, or the next day . . .

Rantor's reverie was broken by a cry from the masthead lookout.

'Land! Land on the port bow!'

He leaped into the shrouds, and, shading his eyes against the sun, looked out across the sea. After the winds of the past few days, the ocean was still heaving in a long swell, but he automatically adjusted his balance to the swaying rhythm. At the height of the roll, as the bow lifted, and hung, momentarily, before plunging back down into the trough, he caught a glimpse of something that might have been the top of an island. Damn the lookout! If land was visible from the deck already, he should have seen it long ago, from his vantage point. But, Rantor realized, like everyone else on the ship the lookout had been more engrossed in Hawk's antics than in his own duties. Damn the Hawk!

He opened his mouth to curse the lookout aloud, but closed it again. Bryon had appeared as if by magic at Rantor's side; it was the Captain's job to discipline the crew, and it was also, to some extent, Rantor's fault for permitting the distraction, when he knew they were approaching land. There was no need for words between them; both he and the Captain knew the situation.

'Douse that fire! All hands!'

The thunder of feet on the planking of the deck broke the silence that had followed the lookout's cry.

Bryon turned to Rantor. 'An outlying island. The new archipelago must still be a day's sailing away. But there are no ships to be seen. No harm has been done.'

The words were scarcely out of the Captain's lips when they were contradicted by events.

'Birds! Two great birds, ahead!'

As if to atone for his previous failure, the lookout had spotted something totally unexpected. They were still too far from land to expect to see birds. Yet there were two dots in the sky, between the ship and the strange island. They could only be birds, but the lookout had done well to spot them.

Rantor felt a thrill of anticipation. Birds meant that the land was alive. Where there were birds, there would be plants – food, and maybe people. *This* was what the *Far Trader*'s voyage was all about. Hawk's toys, and his philosophizing, were all very well in their place. But they could not compare to the prospect of discovering new lands, for the first time in the history of the Archipelago. If nothing else, they could replenish their diminished supplies, provisioning the ship for further explorations. And at best – who knew what the inhabitants of the new islands might have to trade?

In response to shouted orders from the Captain, the ship had altered course towards the lone island, and, with all sail now set, she was heeling slightly even in the fading breeze. Rantor shifted his position, maintaining balance without thinking. His eyes still peered intently at the scene ahead. There was something odd about those birds. Either they were much closer than he had thought, or they were *very* big, and still some distance away. And why did their wings not flap? They seemed curiously stiff, gliding through the air with outstretched wings. The glide-eagles back home soared that way, in the updrafts of wind along the clifftops; but they never held their wings quite so straight for so long – certainly not out in the middle of the sea, where there were no up-draughts. And whatever they were, those two birds *were* coming out to sea, towards the *Far Trader*.

Hawk joined them on the after deck. He seemed entirely

oblivious to the new developments, and was chattering away excitedly, as much to himself as to anyone else.

'A great success! I believe I have the answer. Did you see how pieces of paper float upward in the heat, even when they are not on fire themselves? It all seems quite clear to me. Like attracts like, that is obvious – a law of similarities. Hot things are drawn to the sun, and rise upwards. Cold things, of course, are repelled from the sun, uniformly in all directions, and spread out evenly over the surface of the inner sphere. Which is why all the water doesn't slop down and drown the Islands. What will the priests make of this, eh?

'But the cold things repel the sun, with equal but opposite strength, and push it to the centre of the inner sphere! If we could weigh the brazier, it would surely be lighter when the coals are glowing red, although it has too much inherent weight ever to float in the air. But the paper is so light that even warm air, rising to greet the sun, can carry it along. Ah, Navigator, this is a great day – and one you will remember. I think I can put land and sea breezes at your disposal, now I have this new perspective on things. It's all to do with the law of similarities. Hot air, moving to greet the sun . . .'

'Not now, Hawk.' The Navigator's firm command cut off the flow of unheeded talk. 'What do you make of those birds? A little big, do you not think? Are they a danger?'

Even as Hawk looked up, taking notice of what was going on for the first time, a new cry came from the lookout.

'Men! Not birds! Flying men! Men with wings!'

※   ※   ※

The hiss of the Dream fire being damped down brought Elyse back to reality. That really had been one of the strangest visions; her own fire leading her into a Dream, with another fire in the Dream itself, a focus for strange thoughts and ideas. She shook her head, eased some of the all-too-familiar stiffness from her limbs, looked around.

Gregor, bless him, had left water on the table by her side, some cheese, a little bread. She drank, then ate, while she tried to get the new ideas straight in her head. But, try as she might, they stayed tangled.

The ship had been familiar enough, and some of the people on board she could now recognize from repeated Dreaming. But the fire was incomprehensible. Why would anybody want to build a fire on board a ship? And the images still lingering in her head, of globes like fishing floats, but half-filled with water, made no sense at all.

She shivered, suddenly, clutching her arms to her body for warmth. Suppose someone else shared her Talent! Suppose the fire on board that ship had been built to help someone Dream about her! She'd accepted for some time now that the events she saw in her Dreams were real – but she'd never before imagined that those real people might Dream about her. The thought passed. It was ridiculous; they were all men on board the ship, and only women could be blessed with a Talent. And surely she would have known, if she were sharing the thoughts of another Firedreamer in the midst of a Dream?

The door behind her opened, quietly. She turned her head, smiling at the broad figure of the blacksmith, Karyn's brother.

'Awake, then?' Gregor had a habit of stating the obvious.

She nodded. She could put up with any amount of obvious questions in exchange for Gregor's quiet acceptance of her, his willingness to give her a home, treating her as if she were his own sister returned to the village, and not an outcast stranger. And the smithy was an excellent base for a wise woman – a centre of village life where gossip was exchanged and troubles were aired. She'd really fallen on her feet here. But she had to earn her keep.

The Talent was proving as useless as ever. The strong Dreams of the Ship (she'd begun to think of it with a capital S) were as overwhelming as ever, but offered her no clues as to how to improve the lot of poor farming folk. On the other hand, the fact that she unmistakably *did* Dream, seeing strange visions in her fire smoke and falling into a trance from which nothing could rouse her until the Dream was over, itself cemented her position in the village community. The villagers didn't need to know *what* she was Dreaming, as long as they knew that she was a true witch, expelled from the Halls, sent by the Fates, no doubt to replace their own Karyn. And though some might mutter that it was a pity she didn't have young Karyn's way with plants, so far the advice she had been able to give them, based on Halls Knowledge and her own quick wits, had been enough to maintain her place in the community. She might even have grudgingly acknowledged, had there been anyone to ask her, that there might after all be some wisdom in the idea of sending Sisters with worthless Talents back into the community, to share their Knowledge and more everyday skills with those who had not had the benefit of a Halls upbringing. But she would *never* acknowledge that sharing her wisdom, such as it was, must necessarily involve the loss of her Talent, feeble though it was. Which made Gregor's clearly brotherly care for her all the more welcome.

'Have you any advice for the Council?'

She nodded again. She'd had the advice clear in her mind, of course, before she had built up the fire, added the fresh twigs, and settled down to gaze into the smoke. She had no intention of claiming that her advice came from the Dreams; but if the villagers chose to believe that, then so be it. The problem was simple enough. Although there was still water in plenty available from the Great River, it was arduous work getting it to the crops, and the lack of clouds, day after day, allowed the sun to wither and burn them. She knew part of the answer, which had already been worked out by the Seniors in the Halls (for all she knew, with the aid of someone's genuine Talent) in the face of the much worse drought being suffered inland from Seahaven. She'd heard the problem discussed; but the solution hadn't yet been put into practice at the time she had left. There was no way the news could have outrun her.

'They must collect forest litter. Leaves, twigs, even small branches. Spread them among the crops. They will protect the soil from the direct heat of the sun, and trap the dew at night, so that it will soak into the ground.'

'That's all?'

She smiled. 'That's all for now, Gregor Smith.'

'It seems too easy. Obvious.'

'So why hasn't anybody done it before?'

The question was unanswerable. And by the time news

75

came from the west about the value of this obvious trick, that would only enhance her reputation, as the villagers would be able to tell the messenger, 'Oh, *that* old trick – we've been doing it here for many seasons. Isn't it obvious?'

He nodded, thoughtfully, thinking it through.

'And young Bjarni?'

Here she was on even more solid ground. When it came to settling the day-to-day disputes in the village, she only had to put herself in Sister Senior's shoes, and make a suitable pronouncement. The villagers' respect for her Halls wisdom did the rest. The fact that she was almost certainly not quite as old as 'young Bjarni' would make no difference, she knew – at least, as long as she kept making the right decisions. And she knew *exactly* how Sister Senior would respond in this situation.

'He must marry the girl. His brothers must help him to build a house, by the river, where there is easy access to water. And if the baby is a girl, then in due time she will be my apprentice.'

That one pierced even Gregor's impermeability to surprise.

'But witches – I beg your pardon, Elyse, but . . .'

'Witches don't have apprentices, Gregor Smith? Well, this one intends to. How else will the village have anyone to look after it when I'm gone? And don't talk to me about Talents. There's more to being a wise woman – or even a witch – than Talents, you know. Not,' she added thoughtfully, 'that you need tell anyone I said so.'

The big man was silenced. Well, it would do him good to be taken by surprise. She didn't want *anyone*, least of all Gregor, to find her too predictable. And why shouldn't she have an apprentice, or two? She could never rival the

Halls, but she could do something to establish a permanent pool of wisdom here in the Eastern Settlements, if her luck held.

❋   ❋   ❋

As the flying figures swooped towards the *Far Trader*, a murmur ran round the crew. Several of them made the sign to ward off evil. The older hands turned to the Captain for orders. Hawk, attention well and truly caught, ran the length of the deck and scrambled up into the rigging, staring forward. As the ship rolled, he lost his grip with one hand, and swayed out over the heaving waters; but he kept his eyes fixed on the fliers as he scrabbled for a secure grip. Rantor had the feeling that even if Hawk fell to his death he would spend the fall observing his surroundings, and thinking about what it all meant.

'Prepare for boarders!' The Captain, as ever, thought first for his ship. 'Men or birds, they don't come aboard the *Far Trader* without my invitation, lads!'

The rough humour turned the mood of the crew away from thoughts of black magic. They had the best Captain in the Archipelago, *and* the best Navigator – and they had their own secret weapon, the Hawk.

The two swooping figures split up to pass either side of the ship, as crossbowmen hurriedly took up positions by the rail. Hawk slid down a rope and scurried back, keeping pace with the fliers.

'Men indeed, Captain,' he panted. 'Not birds. Ordinary men like us. See the harness that fastens them to the wings. But see how they fly – like eagles.'

The two fliers had indeed soared high over the ship, having used the momentum of their dive, as they crossed the stern and turned back to pass the vessel, to lift them higher. But not quite like eagles. Their wings did not flap, and now they were sinking, slowly, towards the waves.

'I think not, Hawk.' Rantor had grasped their difficulty. 'These eagles will never regain the land. How they rose so high in the sky, I know not. Perhaps it was the attraction of the sun, eh? A wonderful trick for a lookout – but they should have stayed closer to home. Now they are sinking lower. We may have two passengers for you, Captain – and wet passengers, at that.'

Suddenly, one of the fliers, now only a few span above their heads, veered to his right, towards the ship, losing height as he did so. The small group on the after deck flung themselves flat as his intentions became clear. For a moment, it looked as if he would succeed in landing on the deck. Then, the left wing snagged a standing line, part of the permanent rigging. There was a snap, and the whole wing crumpled, while the flier himself was jerked around and crashed heavily into the rail. Bryon and Rantor, with two crew members, rushed to his aid; Hawk moved with equal speed, but ignored the man and poked gently at the broken wing, no more than a delicate framework of wood covered with fine silk. It had scarcely more substance than the wing of a butterfly – and yet it had carried a man high above their heads, and brought him all the way here from the island ahead. A strange-looking man, he was dressed in what would have been loose trousers, except for the thonging binding them tight around his legs, and a jerkin that left his arms bare. Beardless – that was almost unheard of back in the Islands – and he met Rantor's gaze steadily with blue eyes, not brown. A man for all that, who bled like any mortal man.

A splash alongside, accompanied by a slightly inaccurate cry of 'Man overboard!', announced that the other butterfly had come to the end of its flight. Bryon left the others attending to the injured flier – his arm seemed to be broken, and he was only semi-conscious.

79

'Get a line to him, then!'

In response to the 'man overboard' cry, the helmsman had immediately hove to, and the flier, already disentangled from his wings, was struggling in the heaving water alongside. The wind had scarcely increased during all the activity, and in spite of its modest headway the ship was still comfortably close enough for a line to be heaved to the swimmer. He soon stood, panting, on the main deck. Rantor went to greet him, only to be taken aback by the flier's words.

'I hope you fools are worth the trouble.' The accent was peculiar, but intelligible. 'My wings lost, because your idiot crew were too busy saving me to think about them; Bah-lee's wings probably smashed beyond repair. And all because you weren't prepared to receive us properly! Don't you know the Code? Someone will have to pay for this mess!'

'We hardly expected such visitors, ah,' the Navigator decided to be tactful, 'Lord. Indeed, we have never seen such wonders as men that fly.'

'I am no lord.' The visitor was looking about him. 'But where are you from? There is no ship like this in the Nations. All these ropes, and poles. And such a mess of sails. Where are your oars? Why is there no clear deck for fliers to land on?'

'We have oars – when we need them.' The Navigator looked at Bryon, and nodded.

The Captain took the hint. The weak breeze was getting them nowhere now, and it began to look like a good idea to make land as soon as possible. A few quiet commands, and the ship was bustling with activity as sails were taken in, and, to the accompaniment of good-natured complaints from the men who would have to heave on them, oars were unshipped. The flier, drying in the warm sun, watched with obvious interest. The men labouring at the sweeps held so much fascination that, Rantor surmised, this was not the kind of oarsmanship the man was used to. Irritated at the flier's manner, he tried, once again, to gain his attention.

'But, as I said, we have never seen men that fly.'

This time, the flier took it in. His attention jerked back to Rantor.

'Never seen fliers? Then you are strange fish indeed, and King Rotono-ga will surely regard you as a catch worth even the cost of two sets of wings! Keep on this course, and I will take you into harbour.'

Rantor frowned. He objected to being regarded as a catch. It was a long time since anyone had given *him* orders. But he had every intention of taking the ship into harbour – not just for supplies, but for the secret of the flying wings. And he never objected to the help of a local pilot. If this ill-mannered passenger wanted to think he was in charge, it was best to allow him that illusion, for now.

FIVE

As the hands of days passed, Elyse became aware that she was becoming accepted as part of the village scenery, an object of pride — few villages had their own wise woman, one with a genuine Talent, even in these remote settlements, far from the direct influence of the Halls — but also, if she were not careful, at risk of being taken for granted. Her youth, she knew, counted against her. So she stayed indoors a great deal, keeping to the darker corners, and favoured a long brown cloak with a deep hood. This didn't give her much scope for running in the woods, or climbing trees, although she made a point of travelling out to one quiet glade at least every five days to light a fire and make smoke out of the green leaves and twigs. And if sometimes all she saw in the patterns in the smoke were smoke patterns, who was there to know that her Talent wasn't quite so wonderful after all?

At least the ritual gave her time to think. Time to think about the problems of the village; time to recall stories from her girlhood of the strange ways of witches, with a new understanding of their reclusive ways and mysterious secrets. How many of them, she wondered, were as ordinary as herself, clothing themselves in an aura of mystery to preserve their place, such as it was, in the community? And yet she *did* do good, in a small way. If only she could come up with something big. Something big enough to make a lasting impression; something worth weaving into a story for mothers to amaze their children with, and to make sure of her place here, not just for a few hands of days but, if necessary, for a lifetime. But the smoke, for now, refused to help. It was almost as if her security and distance from the Halls had dimmed her power of Dreaming. She had Seen before with full strength when threatened with failure at the Halls; again at the fishing village where she had thought her flight from the Halls had come to an end. Did her Talent need the threat of personal danger to be awakened? If so, how long would it be before Gregor and his friends decided that she might, after all, be of more value working in the fields than hiding in dark corners and offering advice on minor problems of village life?

Gregor. Just how fraternal was his concern for her, anyway? He saw more of her than anyone else in the village, and knew better than anyone else her youth. The way he looked at her sometimes made her feel quite strange; not threatened, but decidedly strange. She must try to remember to keep the witch's cloak about her even when they were alone. *Especially* when they were alone. But, try though she sometimes might, she could not convince her Talent that the prospect of losing her status in the village represented a threat severe enough to bring back the Dreams. She had run as far as it was possible to run; whatever became of her now, it had to happen here.

※　　　※　　　※

How could they have been so stupid! Rantor fumed inwardly. Seventeen days of inaction. A stand-off. The representatives of this cursed King Rotono-ga still demanded that the ship – the whole ship! – be given up in compensation for the loss of two sets of wings that they blamed on Rantor. They could take it by force, of course, here in the harbour; though Rantor would burn it first, and had made sure they knew it. Or they could starve the *Far Trader*'s crew into submission, eventually. That, he thought with grim satisfaction, might take longer than they expected, and he would still burn the ship before they got their hands on it. Rantor had bought time, he hoped, by giving the impression that their supplies were all but exhausted, and he had repeatedly asked for more, without success. That should encourage this King and his men to play the waiting game, at least for a while. But could anything about them be predicted, when the idiots refused to trade!

Maybe they were not such idiots. They held all the best cards, with the *Far Trader* in harbour, under the watchful eyes of the King's men. Eventually, they would be forced to beg for supplies, or try to sail off – and how could you sail off unobserved, even if you could sneak or fight your way out of harbour, when the King had fliers who could scan the seas for a sight of you from above? In the long haul, the *Far Trader* could outpace any rowing galley. But if the rowing-boats knew where she was, and enough of them gave chase promptly, they could quickly catch her.

He'd been a fool to lead them into this mess. Should have

anchored off shore, and negotiated at arm's length. But even then, with those damned fliers, the locals would have been at an advantage. In any skirmish, it would be easy to keep them off the ship's decks – but that would not suffice. A few daredevils, landing in the rigging and cutting it, and the ship would be lost, disabled, while the rowing-boats came alongside at their leisure. The *Far Trader*'s clumsy sweeps, useful though they were for getting in and out of harbour, were no match for purpose-built galleys.

Still, he *had* been a fool to imagine that the whole wide world would be like the Archipelago, only bigger. Back there, there were always different factions, shifting coalitions among the different groups of islands, so a good trader could play one off against the other, and find some way to turn things to his advantage. But here – he could still hardly believe it: a single, big island, isolated in the sea with everyone owing allegiance to a single ruler. There were no factions for him to set one against the other. No real ships, just those glorified rowing-boats – which was why they were so eager to lay hands on the *Far Trader*, now that they had seen the possibilities she represented. The big mountain in the middle of the island made overland travel difficult, but the rowing-boats managed quite well plying around the coast. There were enough experienced sailors here to make copies of the *Far Trader* and to sail them, and Rantor shivered at the thought of what they might do if let loose in the Archipelago. And who could have imagined the fliers? – everything hinged on that.

'Navigator.'

'Hawk! I was contemplating your advice. Trying to find the right viewpoint to tackle the problem of how we get out of here.'

'I may be able to help.'

'Your lightning generator won't get us out of this harbour, friend.'

'No.' Hawk gripped the Navigator's shoulder, and crouched close by his chair, keeping his voice low. 'But if we were at anchor, halfway round the island from here, and if there was a good strong land breeze blowing, and if I could guarantee no fliers could follow you for – oh, half a day, or so – what might your instructions to the Captain be?'

'Cut the cable. Run. With a head start, and no fliers to interfere with the sails, we could hold the rowing-boats off until they tire.' Rantor's eyes were suddenly alight with interest. 'But can it be done, Hawk? Do you really have a plan?'

'Oh yes, Navigator. I have a plan. And I have a secret worth far more to these people than the *Far Trader*. I can show them how to fly at night, and in the first light of morning, when, as you must have observed, their beautiful butterflies must stay on the ground.'

The Navigator sat back, with a sigh. 'A wonderful secret, indeed, my friend. But if you think this will pay for our release, you are sadly mistaken. This King of theirs will take your secret, and keep us, and our ship, into the bargain.'

'But I *cannot* stay here, Navigator. *We* cannot stay here. I have work to do – the theory of similarities has such interesting implications. I *must* have somewhere to work properly again.'

Rantor's hope was quickly fading. The Hawk, he remembered, had come to the Three Islands from a far distant part of the Archipelago. He owed no true allegiance to the Duke; all he wanted was a benefactor who would allow him his experiments. Even the precious ship meant nothing to him, except that it was a rather inconvenient platform for those studies. Yet, Rantor counted him as friend, and believed the feeling was reciprocated. If not through allegiance to the Duke, then surely out of that friendship Hawk would not simply slip away with his new secret, and offer his services to the King?

'We go together, Hawk; or not at all. I'll not abandon *one* of those under my command.'

Hawk ignored, or failed to notice, the hard edge that had entered Rantor's voice.

'To be sure. Of course.' He was losing himself in his dream-world again, muttering almost inaudibly as he went over complex plans in his head. 'Even a King must have his secrets, and my secret is so powerful that it cannot be revealed near the prying eyes of the town. Some distance away, around that headland yonder, would be appropriate. And the ship must be on hand, to ferry my equipment – they won't think that is odd, all the transport here goes by sea.' He stopped, and looked earnestly at Rantor again, as if a doubt had just occurred to him.

'Ah, Navigator, I will need rather a *lot* of equipment. It might be best if you were to explain this to the Captain.'

Rantor had got into the habit of trusting the Hawk. It was a habit he couldn't bring himself to break, although he vowed to himself that if this were some trick he would not rest until the trickster paid.

'The Captain will surely be in accord. Even if the fliers pursue us, it will be better to go down fighting, in the open sea, than to starve here in harbour. At night, with just a few guards to overpower, and the land breeze . . .' he shrugged. 'Well, we won't win. But they'll know they've been in a fight.'

He stopped short. 'But where will you be, Hawk? How can we slip our cable and flee, if you are ashore, demonstrating some flimflammery to the King's men?'

The Hawk's familiar grin returned. 'Flimflammery, Navigator? Have you so little faith? Oh no. My tricks, as you well know, always work. But this one may not work out in the way that other people anticipate. All you have to do is wait a little while offshore, to collect me before you set full sail. I assure you, there will be no fliers to hinder your escape. It all has to do, you see, with the attraction of similarities and the repulsion of opposites.'

Try though he might, that was all the information Rantor could extract from his far-sighted friend. That, and a list of essential equipment for hoodwinking the King's men that made no sense at all. While Captain Bryon only agreed to the assault on his ship's stores on the strength of Rantor's own solemn vow that the result would be, at least, to get the ship out of this damned harbour.

※　　　※　　　※

The flames seemed to leap higher at her approach, sending sparks swirling into the night air. Of course, it was an illusion, Elyse told herself, a trick of perception, caused by her heightened awareness of the power of the flames, and the way the small crowd of people edged gently aside, giving her space, and a clear view. The harvest festival was a muted affair, in line with the modest size of the harvest itself. But there was a harvest, even if it was a modest one, and tradition demanded that it be celebrated in the proper fashion, with bonfire and dancing. If the village failed to maintain the tradition, who could guess how bad the harvest might be next time?

Elyse stared into the fire, willing herself to see something more than the pattern of flames and smoke. As she concentrated, blotting out the surrounding distractions, all she seemed to see was an even fiercer surge of conflagration, accompanied by a louder crackling as the dry — too dry — logs burned more fiercely. And there was another sound, a murmuring from the villagers nearby, who backed ever so gently further away from her. Startled out of her reverie, she glanced around from beneath the cover of her hood. It was *not* an illusion! The intensity of the fire really had increased at her approach, as she concentrated her mind upon the flames — and others had noticed the change.

At least, they thought they had noticed a change. But it wasn't too late to sow doubt in their minds. There was no need to cause more excitement; she could back away now, take a drink of the mulled wine, keep away from the flames, think about *anything* except fire. Nobody would expect her to join in the dancing. Let the fire take its natural course, and in the morning nobody would really believe that the witch had the power to make the fire burn brighter. Anybody who mentioned such a story would be laughed at, in the light of day; anyone who imagined they remembered such an event would tell themselves that it was imagination, the influence of the wine, linking the witch with the fire that she was known to find her visions in. Or a coincidence, caused by a fresh log falling into the heart of the flames as she happened to be approaching.

But she knew. As her Dreams were deserting her, her power over the flames was growing. It wasn't just, as she had thought, that she was getting more skilful at lighting her fires and tending them with fresh-cut branches. The flames really did respond to her wishes. Another useless Talent. The last thing anybody could want in the middle of a drought would be a fire-raiser. This secret she *had* to keep.

She left the celebrations as early as was decent, and retired to bed. There, without the aid of any living fire at all she Dreamed once more, as if her Talent had never deserted her. But although she Dreamed without the aid of fire, once again fire lay at the heart of the Dream.

❊   ❊   ❊

Hawk was tired. It had seemed like a brilliant move on the Navigator's part, insisting so firmly that he could not possibly let his Hawk go into the midst of the islanders unescorted. Of course, Rho-gan, the King's man, had insisted even more firmly – and from a position of inarguable strength – that nobody except the Hawk was to leave the ship. Hostages, instead, were offered against the Hawk's safe return. Even now, Bah-lee, his arm in splints, sat in the Captain's cabin on board the *Far Trader*, guarded by the crew. The ship in turn was watched over by more of the King's men, in their 'rowing-boats'.

There was no point in worrying about it now, but if it hadn't been essential for Rantor's bluff to succeed, Hawk would have welcomed the presence of someone he could really trust, here to help him with the labour of setting everything up. It had been a long and lonely haul from the beach, almost a thousand paces; uphill and inland. The spot seemed almost perfect, and the sea breeze that still blew fitfully on their backs as they manhandled the materials upward had almost died away. The pyre was already well alight.

'Rho-gan!' The islander turned at the Hawk's call. 'Now the wind is dropping, we can begin. Get them to build the fire higher, and to keep the neck of the skysail above the rising smoke.'

'As you command, O Hawk.' Rho-gan was used to giving orders, not to taking them; but he seemed to prefer to amuse himself with mock-obsequious obedience rather than to allow the situation to upset him. This fitted well with Hawk's instructions from the Navigator – escape, by all means, and demonstrate that the crew of the *Far Trader* (and, by implication, the people of the Archipelago) were not to be trifled with. But leave the way open for trade, on more equal terms, later. There was no point in being too secretive about what he was up to and it always calmed his nerves to explain things.

At Rho-gan's instruction, the men with the uncomfortable task of holding the circular mouth of the skysail over the fire had moved a little closer to the flames. The opening was supported on poles, above the fire itself, with each pole held by an uncomfortably hot man; and the neck of the device stretched on more poles from the mouth to the body of the skysail, swelling and stirring on the hillside above like a giant beast awakening from slumber.

'You see how the smoke and sparks rise in the warm air. This is a natural law, the repulsion of opposites. Hot things cannot abide the cold ground, and must rise up above it. My little skysail will do the same.'

'Little!' Rho-gan glanced at the billowing fabric, the remains of the ship's best fine-weather sail, once flat against the slope of the hillside, but now beginning to take on a life of its own as heat from the pyre was directed into its gaping mouth. 'Why, twenty men could scarce encircle it with arms outstretched. But, no doubt, you have much bigger skysails, on your home island?'

'I have never flown one bigger myself.' Which was certainly true, thought Hawk, and, he hoped, sufficiently misleading for the islander to draw his own false impressions. 'But it is nearly time for my demonstration. As an experienced flier yourself, perhaps you could help me with the harness. It is fortunate indeed that your wing-harness could be adapted to my needs; but the design is unfamiliar.'

They moved around the fire together. Even at ground level, the heat was intense. The skysail was almost rounded now, beginning to show signs of trying to lift off the ground, held down by a wide net around which there were many strong ropes, held by equally strong men.

It worked! Hawk tried to conceal his excitement. Of course it worked. He'd known it would. But although the reality was still a thrill, he had to let them think this was all routine.

'Be careful not to let any sparks catch the sail!' The nearest handler grunted something that might have been an acknowledgement. Hawk decided to leave well enough alone. He had plenty to worry about. Let them make sure the skysail was held in place above the rising air, being repelled from the cool ground as the laws of science dictated.

Rho-gan had the harness ready. Hawk, glad of his small stature, slipped it around his shoulders and looked down as the islander fastened the straps securely about his chest. Above his head, the leather harness was joined to ropes that were threaded around the broad mouth of the skysail. It all seemed secure – too secure, for what he had in mind.

'If I should descend a little abruptly, Rho-gan, I might need to wriggle out of this with some haste, before the skysail falls on my head and smothers me.'

The islander nodded. 'A real problem – should you rise more than a few span above the ground.' Was Rho-gan mocking him? No matter; mocking or not, he was explaining what Hawk needed to know. And the less faith he had in the skysail, the bigger the element of surprise that would help Hawk on his way.

'This knot here can be released by a tug, so –' he demonstrated, then began refastening the harness '– but it is best not to tug it when you are floating far above *our* heads!'

Hawk grinned. He could not help but like this man. Maybe they would meet again. There was much he would like to

93

learn about the flying wings of the islanders. But timing was all important, now. He had instructed the Navigator to make his move when the fire began to die down, as it would as soon as he was safely on his way and the enthusiastic arsonists he had recruited ceased flinging wood on to the blaze. He felt a tug at his shoulders, and the hair rose on the back of his neck. He had never doubted the device would work, but this was a little different from his usual experiments. This time, he was experimenting on *himself*.

He looked up. The skysail was almost over his head, held to one side by the ropes to trap the rising heat from the fire. The ropes to his harness were stretched almost tight. He had to go, and trust the land breeze to appear on schedule. In his mind, he knew it would; but his stomach seemed to be trying to disagree with his mind.

Rho-gan was smiling at him. 'Well, Hawk. Time to live up to your name. A man is not a real man, I always say, without his wings. Your skysail is not my idea of flying. Dangling on a piece of string, unable to steer a course. But I have to admit that my wings would never get me aloft this night, while your skysail seems just as reluctant to have contact with the ground as you foretold. If it takes you higher than I can jump, I'll make you an honorary member of the fliers' guild tomorrow.'

I may not be able to steer a course, thought Hawk, but if it goes where I plan, you'll never get the chance. He smiled in return, with genuine warmth. He hoped Rho-gan would carry no blame for what was about to happen.

'Ready.'

Rho-gan took up the cry. 'Our Hawk is ready to fly! Release the bird!'

Well-disciplined, the men on one side of the network of ropes holding down the skysail released their grip, allowing it to slide out from under the mesh, and rise above the fire.

Jerked sideways, Hawk began to run, then stumbled; for a moment, he thought he was being dragged into the fire. Then, with a bound, the sail was free of the netting, and rose upwards at a giddy pace. His boots barely brushed the flames, and he was aloft, floating in a warm column of air, soundlessly, like a bird.

Time, he knew, was short. Soon, the heat in the skysail would be dissipated, escaping and vanishing into the sky as it was repelled by the cool surface below. As the skysail cooled, then, in accordance with the law of attraction of similars, it would descend gently (he hoped) back to the ground. But it was no use landing back where he had started. Everything depended on the land breeze, the night wind that *always* blew off from the shore to the sea, from every island, the Navigator had assured Hawk, that he had ever encountered.

Hawk knew why it did so, now. Air warmed by the sun's action by day was drawn towards the heat of the sun by the attraction of similars. That was why these island fliers could soar so high on their wings, during the heat of day. The rising air lifted them up. Naturally, since the land was higher up than the sea, it felt the effect more strongly, so the rising air moved up over the sides of the mountain, reaching for the sun.

At night, the pattern was reversed. The air above became cool, when the sun went dark at night. Cool air was attracted back down to the cool surface below, and that attraction was stronger on the high slopes of the mountain. Cold air fell down the mountainside and blew out to sea, as the land breeze.

No wing flier could leave the ground when the land breeze blew; he could fly upward only in rising air, in the heat of the day. Now the Hawk could fly upward even in cold air – simply by making his own warmth! Once he was aloft, though, on this occasion he needed the cold air, falling down the mountainside, to push him out to sea and back to the *Far Trader*. But nothing was happening! He could feel no breeze at all!

Alarmed, Hawk looked down between his boots. He was far above the tallest trees, twenty, thirty – perhaps fifty – span above the ground. The fire was no longer there! Twisting in his harness, Hawk caught sight of it, well to one side. As he watched, it seemed to drift away. He *was* moving! And towards the sea!

Cries from below broke into his thoughts.

'Hawk! Skysailor! How far do you plan to travel?'

He laughed. All was well. The opportunity was irresistible.

'All the way, Rho-gan! All the way back to my ship! And by the time your fliers can rise on their wings, we will be far, far away!'

Rantor himself led the attack, as soon as he judged that the fire on the hill was beginning to die down. He wanted to be in the thick of things, exercising a restraining influence. It was essential that none of the honour guard for their hostage should be killed; he wanted no excuse for continuing bad blood between the Archipelago and this island. The guards, though, were under no such restraint, and although they were fighting on unfamiliar territory this gave them an advantage. But they *must* be overpowered before the two rowing galleys, surely already alerted by the sounds of the scuffle, could take action.

Short clubs had disposed of several of the guards – Rantor only hoped they had not been wielded with too much enthusiasm – and he noted, grimly, that at least three of his own men were down, wounded seriously. But the swordsman in front of him was no novice, and it was all he could do to keep him at bay, while trying to manœuvre the man into a position where one of the sailors could get in a clear blow at him. The sword flicked in low, stabbing at Rantor's groin; he danced sideways, deflecting the blade with a flick of his wrist, and gave way again. Dammit, this man was *good*; where were his helpers?

Suddenly, the *Far Trader* lurched, as the cable was cut and her head began to swing in the breeze. Rantor adjusted easily to the sway; his opponent, clearly a landsman, was caught off balance. Seeing an opening, Rantor lunged forward, aiming to disable his sword arm. To his horror, as the ship heaved his opponent stumbled into the strike. Desperately, at the last moment Rantor managed to lift the point of his blade, which struck high in the man's right shoulder, instead of penetrating deep into his chest. As the wounded man tried to switch the sword to his left hand, two of the crew swung from the rigging, taking him from behind. He sank to his knees, clearly in pain and losing blood fast; but not, Rantor prayed, mortally wounded.

He looked around. The fight was over, and the ship was under way. But there were more problems yet to be faced. Grunting an acknowledgement to his helpers, he ran back to the after deck, absently cleaning the sword on his cloak as he went.

'Steady.' Captain Bryon's quiet command travelled the length of the now silent ship. One of the guard boats was swinging round, under all oars, as if making to board. The other stood off for the moment. 'Now! Hard to port, in oars!'

Swept forward by the press of sails, even with all oars inboard, the *Far Trader*'s manœuvre caught the galley crew, used only to fighting their own kind, off guard. Sliding down the side of the smaller vessel, the *Far Trader* neatly snapped off every oar in turn, leaving the rowing-boat helpless, at least for the time being. Under the Captain's orders, the *Far Trader* turned back on course, heading directly out to sea, but under reduced sail. The other galley paced them easily, at a safe distance, hailing across the gap between the two vessels.

'*Far Trader!* Your hostage will be forfeit!'

Bryon looked at the Navigator, who nodded. The Captain hailed back.

'He must take his chance! But we have some passengers here who would like to join you. We will give them a boat.'

The Captain played out his scene, dawdling along, ostensibly in order to give the prisoners a chance to disembark, and carefully briefed crewmen took as long as possible over the job. All the while, anxious eyes, including those of the Navigator, scanned astern – for any sign of pursuit, or of the Hawk's skysail. Could it really work? A man – even the Hawk – was so much bigger than a scrap of paper. Would he even try to get back, or did he plan to stay on the island, with a new benefactor? For all Rantor knew, another double hand of galleys might be ready for them, just out to sea, waiting to spring a trap.

'I see him! Twenty points on the starboard quarter!'

The Navigator looked to his left. A white blob, shining in the faint light of the nightglow, scarcely a mast's height above the water. And falling fast.

'A crown piece for that man!' The Captain's voice rang clear. 'Cut that boat free! Oars! In sail!'

Turning almost in its own length, the *Far Trader* surged towards the rapidly sinking skysail. Suddenly, the skysail lifted once again, but as it did so a tell-tale splash beneath it told its own story. The Hawk had dropped free, into the water, abandoning his strange craft.

Surprised once again by this new turn of events, the remaining guard boat was a full two lengths behind as a brawny sailor, supported by two of his mates, scooped a dripping Hawk through a rowing-port while the vessel was still under way. At last, the Captain gave orders for full sail, and the ship heeled under the press of canvas, catching the full strength of the land breeze, as it turned on to its proper course, while the Hawk emerged, dripping, on to the after deck.

'So, Hawk.' Bryon turned his attention away, briefly, from the task of screwing the last measure of speed out of his ship. 'Where's my best light-weather sail when I need it, eh?'

Rantor laughed at the expression that crossed Hawk's face. 'Never fear, Hawk. You are worth more to us than a sail.' He clapped his friend on the shoulder, doubly relieved that the Hawk had indeed been true to his word. 'But that skysailing trick of yours!' He shook his head. 'Something to see. A man floating in the air.'

Hawk grinned. 'You should have seen me earlier, Navigator. At least a hundred span high. But it falls so quickly; it can never really compete with the wings of the islanders. A useless toy, now that the element of surprise is gone.'

'That may not be so.' The quiet voice drew their attention to a forgotten figure, standing awkwardly, one arm stiff, by the rail.

'Bah-lee – why didn't you leave with the others?'

He gave a lopsided shrug. 'Our King, my uncle,' he smiled at the little stir his words caused, 'may have underestimated you travellers. I don't understand the Hawk's trick, but I know its value. If one of those skysails could lift a man and his wings, he could cut loose and be in flight with great ease. The King is no fool, and will value this gift far more than the ship which has so skilfully evaded his grasp.'

'Fine words.' Bryon's expression was sour. 'I'll not return to your island, though, for all your fine words.'

Bah-lee was unmoved.

'Our score, I think, is even. It would be safe to return. But you, I understand, are traders, not in the business of offering gifts, even to great kings. And unless I am mistaken, for all your own fine words I believe that this was your Hawk's first flight. An impressive display. In return for the gift of the skysail, perhaps I can educate your Hawk in the skills of the flying wings, that he may fully live up to his name. And then, maybe, you and your people would know that we are civilized, businesslike folk.'

'We welcome your offer, Bah-lee.' Rantor placed his hand on the flier's good shoulder, in a gesture of friendship. 'But we still have no intention of returning to harbour in your island just yet.'

The islander smiled. 'I am not sure how welcome I would be myself just now, after having been fooled so completely. And I would like to learn of these other islands you speak of. My uncle instructed me to gain such information from you as I could, and how better to do so than by joining in your voyaging? Then, when we return, I may have enough value to atone for past errors. While you will have an emissary able to approach the King through, ah, the proper channels.'

Other islands. The words took away all thought of the pursuit, already lagging behind them. Together, the sailors and their guest turned to face out to sea. It was still dark. The nightglow, concentrated around the land, was behind them. Ahead, as their eyes adjusted to the gloom, they could pick out, faintly, other patches of light. Lights in the sky which, they now knew, must be other islands, other archipelagos – other worlds, with their own strange customs. Next time, the Navigator vowed to himself, they would be prepared – for strange habits, new devices, and different points of view.

He turned back to the islander. 'And the Hawk may yet have something to teach you, Bah-lee. You are welcome to join us on our voyage; but it may take more time than you anticipate. If it is in my power, we will return you to your island, I promise –' He turned back to the rail, gazing out into the darkness, imagining the bowl of the inner sphere, with the *Far Trader* crawling over it. Would the repulsion of opposites really hold them safely pressed against that bowl even while they crawled over the top of the sun? There was only one way to find out. Softly, he finished the sentence.

'– but we are travelling the long way round.'

If the observer could be said to feel disquiet, then disquiet was certainly what it was feeling now. It had instructions to cover every imaginable eventuality; it was also, for all practical purposes, immortal and self-repairing. It had only a dim conception of the passage of time as understood by mortal beings, and in consequence its patience was almost inexhaustible.

Almost, but not quite. Even a self-repairing being has some understanding of how many times it has been repaired, how many components have been replaced, and how many aeons have passed. An immortal being that constantly observes the activities of mortal beings can eventually understand, in an abstract way, what the passage of time means to them. And if the immortal being knows that its instructions were laid down by other mortal beings, then it can, gradually, come to appreciate that things may not be developing in quite the way that the writers of those instructions had planned. If it had been told, for example, to await further instructions, it might eventually begin to wonder just how long it was supposed to wait. And whether there was any way to encourage the mortal beings to put forward the long-awaited new instructions.

But none of this affected the efficient running of the observer's systems, nor the constant attention, across the electromagnetic spectrum, for any signs of intelligence, any response to its own regularly repeated signals.

SIX

'Well, witch!' The words were spat out, full of contempt. Bjarni was angry, as he had every right to be. She stood, wind whipping at her cloak, looking down at the neat wooden house, the parched crops in the roughly fenced fields nearby.

'Come to admire your work, eh? Come to see how well we followed your advice? Come to see how easy it is to fetch water from the river to the fields – when the river itself drops away, and you have to clamber down to reach it? Hard enough work for a man. No work at all fit for a woman with child.'

'I'm sorry.' The words were useless, her presence here an insult. Yet she'd hoped to let Bjarni vent his anger on her, face to face, working it out of his system so that he might be more understanding to a wider audience. She could see the path trodden through the caked and drying mud down to the new river level; imagine the girl, Cladine, struggling up the path, with her swollen belly, carrying her share of the water. Imagine the fall, and the terrible aftermath. And all because she had told the couple to live here, by the riverside, where it would be easy to get water! But how could anyone have known that the river level would drop? Except, of course, that that was what witches were for – to know things that other people could not know. And yet, why hadn't the young couple asked for help?

At least she could guess the answer to that one. No supernatural powers were needed to find an explanation.

The couple knew only too well how the villagers had been struggling to get water into the irrigation ditches in time to save at least part of the crop. They hadn't wanted to be a further burden on the community, after everyone had done so much to set them up in their own home. And everyone else, including Elyse, struggling to make the bucket-lift work, had simply not thought to check up on them in the seven days following the dramatic fall in the level of the river.

Which meant that she was a failure as a wise woman, as well as a witch. A truly wise woman, like one of the Sisters, would have called in everyone from the outlying homesteads, concentrating more people on saving more of the main village crops, abandoning the outlying fields, worrying only about ensuring a sufficient harvest for subsistence until the next one. Well that, at least, probably had been achieved, thanks to the bucket-lift. But what of the season after that, and the next one, and all the rest of the seasons that lay in the future?

She looked away from the distressing orderliness of the farmstead below her, up river to the White Mountains themselves, still tantalizingly clad in a streamer of cloud. Cloud that seemed so reluctant to blow down here on the wind with its welcome burden of rain. The Great River itself must surely originate in the White Mountains, although nobody had ever been to find out. On this side of the river was the rough country, densely forested and a home of wild animals. It began more than a day's ride further inland, providing the space on the gently sloping plain, between the forests and the sea, where the Settlements were scattered. About where the forest began, she had been told, in the tumbled terrain of the impenetrable lands, the river narrowed, becoming a torrent racing down between high, narrow cliffs, impassable for any boat. There was no help to be found there. Even here, it would be foolhardy, under normal conditions, to attempt a crossing, although the river did seem a little calmer at its new, lower level. She turned to her right, away from the river, sweeping her gaze over the brown plain, round to the sea itself, sparkling unconcerned in the bright sunlight. The sea never changed. Briefly, the old Dream image of the great Ship, ploughing through the waves, came to her mind. But it was only a memory of a Dream. Wishful thinking. With a Ship like that, she could carry all of these people away from the parched Land, to some other place, some island rich in fertile land like the ones she had seen in her Dreams.

And yet, something about the sea had changed. In all her time in the Settlements, there had been only one visiting boat, carrying news from Seahaven and the Halls. Until now, she had been glad of the lack of contact with the more civilized parts on the other side of the Great River. More chance for her to establish her place in the community; less risk of being discovered and carried back to the fate she had fled from. But now, the lack of visitors seemed more ominous, and in any case she doubted whether she had a place in the community left to preserve. How badly were *they* faring, with rains failing and rivers suddenly falling? Were the Settlements being abandoned to their fate?

Somebody would have to go back to the Halls, to find out the worst, and to seek what help they could provide. A proper boat would have to be built; the little cockleshells the locals used for inshore fishing would never do for the voyage across the mouth of the Great River. But that would take time.

She continued her turn, until she was facing the river once again. But this time she lifted her head, looking over the roof of the little house and across the water itself. Even this far inland, the river was still wide, but she could see the rough forests cloaking the tumbled terrain on the other side. Over there, the wild land stretched almost to the sea; there had never been any point in attempting to cross and make a landing. But even in a cockle-shell, once across to the other side you could drift gently down river and out, around the headland to the fishing villages on the coast on the other side of the estuary. Of course, there would be no way to bring your small boat back up the fast-flowing river. It would be a one-way journey; a waste of time, in the ordinary way of things, which is why nobody had ever tried it. But these were no ordinary times.

'What do you see, witch?' The words were still bitter, but at least he had lowered his voice a little. 'New farmlands, with plenty of water? What shall I do, swim over there and build a new house? And will you bring back my wife and child to keep me company?'

She reached out, touched his shoulder. She wanted to hug him, but she had to maintain what was left of her mystique. Not just for her own protection; for the sake of the villagers, who would work better for the common good if they had hope. His body was stiff to her touch, muscles rigid under her fingers. Then, suddenly, he relaxed completely, dropping to one knee, burying his face in his hands. She moved her own hand to his head, gently stroking the hair ruffled by the wind.

'Nothing can bring Cladine back to you. And it's true that I am not much use as a witch. But maybe there is still something I can do for the living, even if I cannot help the dead.'

He looked up at her, his face marked by the tracks of his tears. 'Better for us if we'd never set eyes on you, I'm thinking.' The words were still harsh, but his voice was soft, his body relaxed. This was simply defiance for his own comfort, not real anger. But it gave her an opening.

'Or better, maybe, if I were to leave now.' He was sufficiently startled for the tears to stop flowing. Clearly he still regarded her as a witch; still thought a witch might be an asset to the village. 'I'll need your help, Bjarni, to make a decision. I need firewood, green stuff if you can find it, and a safe spot to burn it on, away from the buildings. Near the river.' He nodded. She could see that his respect for the idea of witchery still outweighed his disappointment with her. Of course, the fire would be useless; she didn't expect to see anything in the smoke. But Bjarni would spread the tale of her seeking her smoke visions, here at the spot where Cladine had fallen. And when she told the villagers that she must have a boat and supplies to journey across the Great River and on to the Halls themselves, they would respond unquestioningly, mostly eager to believe that she had had a Vision of how to find help, some of them more secretly relieved to see her gone. Whatever their motives, though – and whatever the futility of her fire-raising – she *would* find help. She owed that much to them, for their warm welcome two harvests ago – and to little Karyn, but for whom she might never have left Seahaven.

As the great fire crackled and roared, sending sparks swirling out across the river, Elyse gazed into the flames, imagining that she saw people and ships. She knew it was only imagination; even when she had had her Talent, it worked best on smoke, not flames. Yet she still had some vestige of Talent, or it had twisted in some way into a new shape. Even allowing for the drought, and Gregor's enthusiasm for collecting firewood, this blaze burned much brighter and fiercer than it had any right to.

Gregor. She turned her head, looking at his large, quiet profile, half hidden in the shadows. Now, that *had* been a surprise.

Few in the village had even bothered to feign indifference when she told them she was leaving, and she doubted that they had much faith in her plan to seek aid. Glad though they obviously were to see the back of her, she doubted just how seaworthy a cockle-shell, and how much food, she might have been supplied with if Gregor had not suddenly announced, in tones which brooked no argument, that he would accompany her to Seahaven. He had, he said, a desire to see his sister once again, and in any case there was little smithing to be done if the fields were too dry to plough. So instead of a cockle-shell they had a solid raft, fresh made from timber set aside by Bjarni for the barn that he no longer had any interest in building.

She was glad to have Gregor with her, some protection against the wild animals that were said to inhabit the forest on this side of the river, and far more able than her at manœuvring the unwieldy raft. They could have travelled down river and out into the bay non-stop, but that would have meant travelling part of the way at night, across uncertain waters. So they had merely (*merely!* the thought of how hard even Gregor had had to struggle to bring the raft ashore reminded her how lucky she was to have him along) crossed over to the uninhabited side on the first day, drifting about halfway downstream to the river mouth while Gregor worked the single sweep that acted both to steer and, to a limited extent, propel the raft, tumbling ashore on a narrow stretch of beach, where her fire now blazed.

Maybe she couldn't steer a raft, but at least she was good at making sure they were warm and their clothes were dry after the rough landing. Her gaze returned to the flames, which seemed to leap again in response. But although she was glad Gregor was with her, she was also afraid. His presence was disturbing, in a way that it had never been even when they were alone at the forge. The forge, after all, was in the village, surrounded by neighbours. Here, they were surrounded only by trees and imagined animals.

'What do you see?' His voice broke into her reverie.

'Only flames, Gregor. I told you, I'm not much of a witch. But I can predict that we'll be tired in the morning, if we don't get some rest.'

They settled on either side of the fire, each wrapped in their own blanket. But Elyse, at least, slept very little that night.

Disaster struck as early as the second day of the journey, confirming Elyse's growing conviction in her own ability to bring bad luck everywhere she went. One moment, the raft was sliding swiftly downstream, smoothly in the fast-flowing current; the next, they had rounded a small promontory to be confronted by an unexpected torrent of white water, new rapids that had emerged unexpectedly as a result of the drop in the river level. Elyse clung to the ropes holding their small bundles securely to the raft; Gregor heaved, with little effect, on the sweep, trying desperately to turn the unwieldy craft to shore. He almost made it. Only a few spans away from dry land the raft struck, first sliding over one rock, then levering itself on to another, where it began to rock in the racing current.

'Jump!'

She shook her head, unable, unwilling, to believe the

instruction. Gregor abandoned the sweep and leapt for the little heap of roped-together possessions, landing with an impact that set the raft rocking even more violently. He grabbed on to the rope with one hand, Elyse's arm with the other.

'Jump, now, Elyse! The raft is breaking up! Jump as far as you can towards land, swim the rest!'

He let go of her arm, produced a knife, and began sawing at the ropes around their bundles. She looked around the raft. It was true. The logs were working against one another and on the ropes that held them together. Even as she watched, one of the ropes parted, and the rocking movement became more of a jerky, up-and-down pitching.

He was right. She looked at Gregor. He nodded. Taking a deep breath, she rose into a crouch, facing the shore. Then, timing her leap to an upward jerk of the raft, she jumped out as far as she could.

The water was cold, rough, and white. It filled her eyes, mouth and ears. It soaked her robe, dragging her down. It tumbled her to the side, but as it did so her feet touched bottom. Kicking off from the rocks, floundering forwards, she found herself kneeling in the foam, within crawling distance of dry land. She turned her head back towards the raft, a surprising distance upstream. Gregor was swinging a bundle to and fro, like a pendulum. He was watching to see she was all right, aware of him. She raised one hand in acknowledgement. One last, long swing and he released the bundle. It flew towards the shore, upstream of her; but it would fall in the water. Of course. She had to stop it. She turned, braced herself, and reached out to grasp the sodden bundle as it was swept down past her. It was as much as she could manage. Clinging desperately to its binding, she sat there in the white water, holding on and waiting for Gregor. She never saw how he in turn leapt into the water, abandoning the second bundle to its fate, and scrambled over to haul her ashore.

Shivering with a mixture of cold and shock, she tried to take stock of what they had saved from the wreck. The cords holding the bundle tight had shrunk in the water, forcing Gregor to cut the knots with his knife. He had gone in search of firewood while she tried to arrange things in some sort of order.

The outer wrapping of the bundle was Gregor's sleeping rug, turned fleece inwards; the wool was still dry, and she hurriedly stripped off her wet gown and wrapped the warming fleece around herself. There was a little food, an axe, Gregor's second shirt, nothing of hers. No fire-making equipment.

Gregor's jacket lay where he had dropped it, a pool of damp surrounding it. She felt in the pocket. The tinder-box was there, sure enough, but soaked. The spring-loaded striker was wet, and refused to spark. She held it under her arm, pressed against her body within the warmth of the rug, trying to dry it out while she gathered some green twigs from the nearby forest edge, and a few dry leaves. Then, she tried the striker again. Was there a spark, or was it her imagination? At least she could try.

Settling over her small heap of kindling, she worked the striker repeatedly. A voice in her head said that it was a waste of time, that even if she did succeed in striking sparks from the metal they could never ignite this green stuff, that she would never make fire without tinder. But it was better than just sitting there, shivering and waiting for Gregor.

There were definitely sparks, now. Was that a glow on a leaf? She leaned forward, started to blow, but it had gone. Forget the blowing. She worked the striker again and again, concentrating, consciousness of her surroundings slipping away, attention focused on the stream of bright sparks. There! A glow on a leaf, a tiny, almost invisible hint of smoke. She watched the glow, motionless, eyes half shut, concentrating on the fire. The glow spread, became a tiny flame; a flame which grew, and leapt to another leaf, then on to one of the still-green twigs. The smoke thickened. She leaned back, suddenly very tired. More wood. She felt sleepy, relaxed, content. But she needed more wood.

As if in answer to her unspoken thought, a large hand appeared, gently adding twigs to the fire. She looked up. Gregor had returned, with an armful of firewood. He looked at her. 'A neat trick, witch.'

How much had he seen? Had she really raised fire from nothing – well, practically nothing – at all? The wet tinder-box still lay beside her. Gregor's eyes rested on it, then flickered to the tiny, growing fire, then back to her. She pulled the fleece closer about herself, aware of just how much of her legs were exposed. She started to pull them in, hunching under the rug, then stopped. What was the point?

She smiled up at Gregor. 'It's the one thing I am good at, Gregor, making people warm. Take off that wet shirt; there's a dry one here.'

He looked away, but started to unlace the shirt, pulling it over his head with difficulty as the damp cloth stuck to his back. She added a small branchlet to the fire. It would be consuming whole logs, soon. Gregor was drying his hair roughly with the wet shirt. Her Talent had left her, she was sure, for good. And it had never been much use as a Talent when she had had it. Dreams of ships that didn't exist! The Sisters were right. She watched as

112

Gregor leaned over to pick up the dry shirt. Why had he really come with her on this foolhardy journey? She stretched her right leg, wriggling her toes to ease the pins and needles she had got from sitting in one position too long. Her legs, she was sure, were shapely enough to be attractive, even if her chest might still be too flat for some men's taste.

'Gregor.'

He looked up, met her gaze.

'I'm told that there are other ways to keep warm than with fire.' It was her turn to look away. She could feel the colour rising in her face. 'Perhaps it is time to find out if I am good at doing it that way, as well.'

'But you are a witch.'

She laughed. 'Not much of a witch, Gregor. I'm no good at foreseeing trouble, I only Dream about ships, and in case you haven't guessed I haven't had a proper Vision since the last harvest. What is there to lose?'

He was silent. She looked up again. The shirt was still in his hand.

'Do you know what you are saying?'

'They did teach us *something* about the real world in the Halls. Especially the duties of a probationer who fails to become a senior. I never did like the idea of the Sisters choosing a mate for me, breeding failed witches like farm animals. But if I am free to make my own choice, that might be a different matter.' She relaxed her grip on the rug slightly. Now her shoulders, as well as her legs, were barely covered by the fleece. For a moment, she thought she had made a mistake. That Gregor really had come along simply in order to visit his sister, not out of any concern, or stronger feeling, for her. Was she even going to be a failure at this?

Then he smiled, tossed the shirt gently in her direction.

'In that case, I'd better build up this fire of yours. Don't want it going out again while your attention is distracted. If you put the shirt on, you can spread that sleeping rug out like it's meant to be.'

He turned his back on her, carefully building up the fire, taking his time. She stood up, dropped the rug, pulled the large shirt over her head, then turned to spread the fleece on the smoothest piece of ground. Then she lay back, tugging the shirt down. It nearly reached her knees. She turned on her side. Gregor still had his back to her, feeding unnecessary sticks on to the burgeoning fire. She smiled. I could have done a lot worse, she thought. Failed witches don't usually get much choice. Then she spoke, softly.

'Gregor.' He stopped feeding the flames, but didn't turn. 'I'm ready to try out the other way to keep you warm, if you can tear yourself away from the fire.' Then, he turned.

In the days that followed, Elyse never once regretted abandoning her Talent and accepting her womanhood. It only took them as long as two days to travel across the back of the headland, through the scrubby woods, because they didn't press themselves to hurry, telling each other that it was best to save their energy against future emergencies. And even without the last vestige of Talent, fire-raising proved no great difficulty armed with dry tinder and metal; she seemed to have got the knack of handling fire, anyway, just as many people who had no pretensions to Talent often had. And with fire, there was no risk from any forest animals that might have ventured this close to the sea, far from the White Mountains.

But Elyse did, very soon, have doubts about whether she had ever been wise to use her Talent in the first place. The success of her ideas concerning sailing against the wind were plain to see as soon as they entered the fishing village, where every boat now seemed to be equipped with what Nathan and his fellow fishermen were calling weather boards – because, as he explained, they made the boats move towards the wind and weather, instead of always running away from it. There was an air of comfort – not exactly prosperity, but certainly not poverty either – around, and the lack of any obvious surprise at her reappearance dressed in a female robe and with what she saw could only be described as a handsome blacksmith in tow, together with a few discreet giggles that she overheard, made it clear that the 'secret' of her disguise as a boy had not lasted long after Nathan had returned home, having delivered her across the mouth of the Great River.

The prosperity, such as it was, depended upon trading fish with Seahaven, and there was no difficulty about arranging passage, with no question of payment being asked from somebody clearly seen as a benefactress. She half-wondered, indeed, whether she might not have done better to be more open with these people in the first place, and to have stayed here all along; but it was so very close to the Halls, and they had indeed told her how riders from Seahaven had twice been by, inquiring after a missing girl. And if she had stayed, she might have had her present agony inflicted on her more often.

Her previous voyage had been straightforward, the boat running before the wind over a gentle sea. But this time, once she had conveyed some idea of the urgency of the position in the Settlements, Nathan had insisted, after making arrangements for a cousin to head back across the Great River to offer what help the village could, in setting out for Seahaven at once, into the teeth of a fierce breeze, and across a wildly broken sea. Thanks to the weather boards, the *Merry Too* was indeed running diagonally into the wind, and almost directly into the lumpy waves. Gregor, like Nathan, seemed impervious to the motion, which only made her feel worse. She sat in the bow, where the wind blew freshest past her face, oblivious to the wet spray soaking her every time the boat thumped into the next wave. When she sat still and upright, it was almost tolerable. Then, some sideways jerk would send her retching, head over the side. And once her head went down, she felt ten times worse, heaving emptily until the spasm passed and she could *gently* lift her head upright again, while clinging on to the rope running from the bow up to the top of the mast.

Gregor sat with her, sharing the discomfort of the open bow, even if he didn't share her misery. And all the time, she kept on thinking how if only she had never had her Dreams this boat would never have been able to take her on this tortuous trip.

Eventually, as the wind fell and backed a little, while the sea eased into a steady swell instead of the vicious chop, she fell into a half-sleep, resting against Gregor, enveloped in his protecting arm. With the motion of the boat, and the nature of the bitter thoughts she had had running through her mind during her sickness, it was hardly surprising that she dreamed, or day-dreamed, of the Ship, even if proper Dreaming was now beyond her. The familiar faces that had once seemed so real to her, and the tall masts of the Ship at anchor (obviously her mind was wishing that the *Merry Too* was at anchor) were clearly Dream memories; the smell of the sea and the feel of the wind on her cheek were all too real, not Dream at all, but built into her Dreaming.

It was in this state, exhausted, beginning to feel hunger

116

but still doubtful about the prospect of eating, thirsty, half asleep, that Elyse was suddenly aroused by a cry from Nathan as the small boat opened the entrance to the Little River, revealing the approach to Seahaven and the safe anchorage in front of the town. She looked up, and back along the length of the boat, under the bottom of the sail, to where he stood, one arm wrapped around the tiller, the other flung out to point ahead. Gregor was asleep. He stirred a little as she turned, digging him in the ribs, and looked forward, following Nathan's pointing finger.

It was a ship. Was she still asleep? It looked just like the Ship she had been dreaming about, riding peacefully at anchor under bare masts. She rubbed at her eyes with her fists, suddenly awake, looked again. No. No dream. It was *the* Ship. The Ship of her Dreams, come to life just as she had abandoned Dreaming. What could it be doing here, in Seahaven? Would the Hawk and the Navigator be here too, or were they just Dream figments? Suddenly she knew, as she had never truly known before, that they were real. How she knew, she could not say; but the certainty made her stomach flutter.

'Gregor!' She shook him, roughly. 'Gregor! Wake up. We're there. And so is my Ship. Now we'll find out what's going on.'

It was the big man's turn to rub sleep from his eyes, stare out from the bow of the boat. He seemed only mildly impressed when he turned his eyes back to her.

'So, it's a ship. A mighty big one, I grant you that. But it's just a ship.'

'No, Gregor, don't you see!' She was kneeling in the wet bottom of the boat, gazing intently into his eyes, willing him to realize the importance of what was happening. 'I told you, when I was a proper witch, before I even came to the Settlements, I used to Dream about a Ship. One of those Dreams showed me how to make a boat sail against the wind – the very trick that has brought you here today. And that –' it was her turn to fling out a pointing finger '– is the very Ship I used to Dream about. I can prove it. Her name is the *Far Trader*. The Captain's name is –' she groped for a moment, then it came to her '– Bryon! But he isn't in charge, the Navigator rules over all. And they have their own Dreamer, a kind of male witch called the Hawk. I know it all, Gregor, don't you see?'

He looked out ahead once again, then back at her, thoughtfully. Gregor was not an impulsive man. Even his decision to come with her on this trip had clearly been premeditated, and was probably the culmination of a genuine plan to visit his lost sister that had been brewing in his mind for all these seasons since she had entered the Halls.

'We'll soon see if this is your Ship, love. Not that I doubt you, but we'll soon find out. The town'll be buzzing with news. But there's no need to let on about your special Knowledge. No need to tell the Sisters you're back, until we're good and ready. Until we know a bit more about what goes on here. Your Ship can't help bring the rain, that's for sure. And it might be keeping the Sisters too busy to do much to help us either. Best to make haste slowly, I'm thinking.'

She saw the wisdom of his words. No, a ship, even *the* Ship, couldn't help to feed the hungry people in the Settlements. She remembered: the Ship needed provisions from the shore to feed its own hungry mouths; that would be why it had put in at Seahaven. The equivalent of another hungry village to be fed, leaving less to help out all round. As for bringing the rain back, not even the

Hawk would be able to do that. She sank down against Gregor again, huddling close for warmth. He was right. They should find somewhere to stay, get all the news. She was so lucky to have him. And when they knew just how things stood, with the Ship and in the Land at large, then they could approach the Sisters with their plea for help. And she already had half an idea how best to make that approach . . .

The Audience Hall was crowded with supplicants, lining the long benches. Across an open space sat three Sisters on tall, high-backed chairs behind a large table. Sister Speaker, of course; the best communicator in the Halls, and a good listener, too, in spite of her name. Sister Senior, also of course, since any important decisions must involve her, and today it seemed that every decision was an important one. And Sister Tutor; a surprise, but only at first sight. Looking out from well back under the hood of her robe, Elyse decided that it was the presence of the strangers that had brought Marretta, as she used to be, here. Naturally, her skills as a teacher also made her a good learner, just as Sister Speaker was also a good listener. And there was, surely, plenty to learn from the people from the Ship.

Turning her head slightly, she could see them, in the row in front of her and Gregor, but some way to their right. Both the Navigator and Hawk, a clear sign, to her who knew them so well, of the importance they attached to this audience. And yet, it was equally clear to her that they were outraged at being made to wait with the other petitioners to present their case, and were barely keeping their patience in check. She smiled under the hood. No doubt they had learned a lot on their travels, not least from the bird men. Here, they seemed determined, in spite of everything, to be on their best behaviour, to fit in with the customs of the Halls.

She had not wasted the four days she and Gregor had spent in Seahaven before this audience, and knew that the sailors had, as tradition required, already met Sister Speaker when handing in their petition, just as Gregor had already spoken to the Sister about conditions in the settlements to the east. Like all the other petitioners, they were here now to receive the response of the Sisters to their various pleas. She could guess what the Navigator wanted – food and water for his Ship. The Hawk would want information, which he was taking in avidly even now, darting glances around the Hall.

The Ship people had, she calculated, been carefully placed in the hierarchy of petitioners. Not first, which would upset important people in Seahaven and might give them an inflated idea of their own importance; but very high up. Gregor had been placed surprisingly high in the queue, not far behind the strangers; a sign that the Sisters regarded him as an emissary from all the Eastern Settlements, perhaps. His ranking today certainly owed nothing to her presence. They had mentioned her background to no one, and Nathan had set sail for home as soon as his cargo of fish had been landed. Throughout the initial audience with Sister Speaker she had sat silent under her hood; she was known to the Sisters, at present, simply as Gregor's companion. And he, as yet, had not even tried to make contact with his sister, Karyn, for fear of her inevitable mention of Elyse. There would be time enough, soon, for her to make her own contribution to the proceedings.

Meanwhile, the decisions being handed out to the eminent petitioners from the lands around the Little River themselves showed how serious things were becoming, even close to Seahaven. All the disputes seemed to involve irrigation rights from the river itself; the simple pleas for help all echoed the word 'drought'. And here was another subtlety in the reasoning of the Sisters – by the time the Navigator received his answer, he would be in no doubt as to the poverty of the Land, and the inability of the Halls to reprovision his Ship.

The moment came. As each petitioner heard the answer of the Sisters, they left the Hall, with the rows of supplicants sliding along the seats to keep the front bench always full. Now, the Navigator and Hawk were at the far left of the front bench; Gregor and Elyse were almost at the right hand end of the same row, and she could not see them at all without craning forward and drawing attention to herself. But she could see Sister Speaker, on behalf of the Halls – on behalf of Seahaven and the lands beyond – delivering the decision.

'Navigator Rantor.' The Sister's voice was soft, pleasing as always. Her message must have been less pleasing to his ears. 'We welcome you and your crew to the Land, as we welcome all strangers. While you are here, we will do our best to be hospitable. But as you see, we are hard pressed to feed our own people. We hope that you will not stay long, and we have nothing to spare to provision your Ship.'

'No!' The Navigator was standing, a clear breach of etiquette. But, as a stranger, this could be forgiven. 'We have nowhere to go, I tell you. Back the way we came, south, it is many days to the nearest island. We were lucky to make landfall here before our supplies were exhausted. And this Land of yours stretches as far as we have been able to check, both west and east. We cannot sail overland. We must have your help if we are ever to leave this place.'

'We have only your word for any of this, Navigator.' The Sister raised her hand to still another outburst. 'Nobody accuses you of lying, but we know nothing of the islands you speak of. It is more natural to suppose, as many do, that you come from a distant part of our own Land, far to the east or the west. And even if that is not the case, you can surely travel either way along the coast, stopping for supplies as soon as you find somewhere free from the drought that afflicts us. You have heard many petitions already today; some among those petitioners might well feel that, with your ship to take you to fertile country, you are better off than they are.'

'Sisters, I beg you.' The Navigator was still on his feet, but he had moderated his tone. 'We have journeyed too far to turn back, even if we had supplies. Help us, and we will give you any help we can in return.'

'How can you help us?' He was silent. By now, Elyse was craning forward, watching the two strangers intently, like everybody else in the Hall. It seemed for a moment that Hawk was about to respond, then he sat back in his seat, turning his eyes to the ceiling.

'If you cannot help us, we cannot help you. We must ask you to leave at the end of the next fiveday. Unless one present here will vouch for you.' The last sentence was a formality, part of the ritual of Audience. It was not intended to be taken seriously.

Elyse rose, pushed back her hood.

'I will vouch for them.' All eyes turned to her, as the clear voice rang round the Hall. 'I will vouch for the Navigator, for the Hawk,' she saw the little man start forward again on the bench, fixing her with his intent gaze, 'for Captain Bryon and all who serve Lord Kyper in the good ship *Far Trader*, and even for their guest, Bahlee the flier.' She was enjoying this. She especially liked the way in which the Navigator and Hawk responded to her list of names, names that, clearly, as she had guessed, they had not mentioned to anyone during their time ashore. 'And I know something that even the Navigator himself does not know, although his friend Hawk very nearly decided to tell you himself, a moment ago. With Hawk's help, these Ship people may indeed be able to come to our assistance, and bring back the rain.'

Suddenly, she wasn't enjoying being the centre of attention quite so much. She sat, but kept her hood back, her gaze fixed on Sister Speaker. But the response came from Sister Speaker's right – from Sister Senior herself, who *never* spoke at an Audience.

'Welcome back to the Halls, Elyse. I was wondering when you would feel it timely to make yourself known to us.' Could she *really* have penetrated Elyse's disguise? Her cheeks flushed at the thought. No, surely it was an Eldest trick, to put her off her guard.

'It seems we are not to continue with our Audience today.' A murmur rose from the petitioners still waiting their turn, but it faded as Sister Senior continued to speak. 'But nobody will begrudge that, I am sure, if there really is a way to bring back the rains, and to solve all our problems. I will speak first with Elyse, alone. Then with Navigator Rantor, his companion, and, ah, Gregor, is it not?' The tall blacksmith rose, and nodded. 'While you are waiting, Gregor, I believe one of our younger Sisters may be available to talk to you. Sister Green – who used to be known as Karyn.' He sat again, a broad smile spreading across his face.

Hall guards were already moving forward, urging the petitioners to leave; Sister Speaker was moving around the table towards the Navigator and Hawk, intent on keeping them occupied for the time being. Sister Tutor, with a smile to Elyse, came up to Gregor, placed a hand on his arm, and urged him to his feet and towards the door at the end of the Hall behind the Sisters' chairs. He glanced at Elyse, who smiled (she hoped reassuringly) and nodded assent.

That left Sister Senior alone at the table. Elyse looked towards her, smile fading from her lips, as the bustle in the Hall died and doors closed solidly behind her. Now, she really would have to come up with a good story. All she had to do, in the next few hands of heartbeats, was work out what it was that had gone through Hawk's mind in that moment before he leaned back and looked with such interest up at the ceiling. But the Eldest didn't look very angry with her. As Elyse watched, the Sister raised her right hand, beckoning her forward.

'Come, child. Sit by me. And explain yourself.'

'. . . and so, Sister, here we were, ready to ask for your help, but I wanted to know more about the Ship and the people of my Dreams, so I didn't make myself known to you. But you knew me anyway?' It was only a half-question. As she had sat, sideways in her seat, recounting her tale to Sister Senior, her old awe of the woman had partly returned. The way she sat quietly, nodding and taking everything in, but giving the impression that she had known it all already, was as impressive as ever. *Had* she known it all already?

'Well, Elyse. I see I should call you "child" no longer. You have done well. But did you really think that I would be surprised to see you here in company with someone from the Eastern Settlements? Especially in the company of a certain blacksmith?'

Elyse flushed. The Sister could still make her feel like a stupid Novice.

'How could you have known where I went?'

'Who was your last visitor, before your untimely departure? And who sent her to you?'

'You mean, you *wanted* me to run away to the Settlements?'

For once, the Sister's air of omnipotence cracked. She actually smiled, shaking her head as she did so.

'Not entirely, my dear.' She had *never* called Elyse 'my dear' before. 'My plans do not always work out perfectly. You should, as you may recall, have had a final Audience with me before leaving; I confess that I had simply been hoping that Karyn might persuade you, in advance, of the wisdom of my decision to send you to the East. Where, as you may have noticed, there is far too little contact with the Halls. And where, if all had gone well, I intended you to settle with a good husband, although I never could have hoped that it would be Karyn's brother.'

'You *wanted* me to go there?'

'Did you never wonder at how easily you evaded capture? At the failure of searchers from the Halls to find a witch girl in a community where gossip is the main source of entertainment?'

'But if, if . . .' she struggled to regain her composure. 'If I had done it your way, I would never have been a witch. Never have been able to tell the fishermen about sailing against the wind, or made the fire.'

'Perhaps not.' The Sister sat there for a moment, thoughtful. Elyse wondered if the private Audience were over. Then she spoke again.

'My dear, it has been a busy day. We have still to discuss your claim that these Ship people can help restore the rains. But I have something else to tell you first, something that you would have learned, before you left the Halls, if you had not been in such a hurry to depart. Something known to all the girls who have left these Halls, and become women; but only to a few of those who stay behind. Only to myself, and Sister Speaker, at present.' She paused again. Elyse tried to guess what might be coming, failed. What secret could she be about to be entrusted with that was hidden from the Sisters themselves, but known to failed Novices, that had never become Sisters? But no guess could have been as bizarre as Sister Senior's next words.

'Why do you imagine that you would have lost your Talent, if you had gone with our approval?'

'Everybody knows, Sister, that a witch is no longer a witch once she has been with a man. I myself, well, I have told you everything.'

'Did you never think this story rather odd? Did you never wonder why this simple physical act should remove your Talent, any more than eating or sleeping should remove your Talent?'

'But, Sister.' She was totally confused. 'Everybody knows . . .'

'Everybody? Everybody who? Everybody outside the Halls, you mean. Everybody that might feel uncomfortable if they had a witch living in their midst. All men. Everybody, in other words, who has no knowledge at all about what they are speaking of.'

'But, do you mean . . .?' It was too much to take in. Could she have Gregor *and* her Talent?

'If there are Novices whose Talents may not be immediately useful here in the Halls, it is natural to send them out into the Land to find husbands. One part of the story is true – women with Talent are more likely to produce Talented daughters than those who have no Talent, and we must always search for new Novices. Husbands from the same bloodline as someone with Talent are always desirable in these cases, which is why I am so pleased about your Gregor. But if someone has a modest Talent that they choose to keep hidden, perhaps doing what good they can without drawing attention to themselves, it might be natural for stories to spread that having a husband meant the loss of a Talent. There is also another small point.'

Sister Senior looked carefully about the Hall, as if checking that nobody had crept in while they were speaking. Her voice, already quiet, became decidedly conspiratorial. 'If men knew that we weak women could be bedded without losing our Talents, how long do you think the authority of the Halls might last? It is those of us who stay here, my dear, not you who go out into the Land, who are making the sacrifice.'

'It cannot be.' She shook her head. How could something she had believed so deeply not be true?

'What, then, did you Dream on the way here, before you saw the Ship in the harbour?'

'I told you. That was just a memory of a Dream. Not real.'

'A memory? Are you sure?'

The picture came back, clear in her mind. The Ship standing at the dock, tall masts bare. Had she ever Dreamed such an image, long ago? She couldn't remember. Perhaps it really *had* been a Dream, while she was cradled, sick and wretched, against Gregor in the boat.

She looked around. As always, there was a fire in the hearth below the great chimney on the western side of the Hall. It was never allowed to go out, although in warm weather it was allowed to burn low, as it was now. She looked back at the Sister. 'May I?' The Sister nodded.

Elyse stood, walked over to the fire. A small bed of glowing charcoal, covered in grey ash, with some sticks smoking at the centre, tiny flames licking along their sides. She picked up a log from the pile on the right of the hearth, held it towards the fire, concentrating hard. She still didn't believe that her Talent could still be with her, but she was determined to give it a good try. She concentrated more fiercely than ever before, remembering the way she had brought the wet tinder to life after the raft wreck, imagining the flames spurting out along the log as it touched the fire, the smoke billowing up the chimney.

Her right hand, holding the log, was becoming uncomfortably warm this close to the fire, even though the fire was so small. She leaned forward, preparing to toss the log into the flames, watching the glowing embers as they seemed to brighten and shine more white than red. Her whole being was focused on the fire, on the warmth of her hand. Suddenly, while the log was still two handspans away from the fiercely glowing embers, it burst into flame. As the heat scorched her hand, she flung the log, with a cry, into the far corner of the hearth, where it blazed even more fiercely than the image she had had in her head, sending not just smoke but flames and sparks roaring into the chimney. Clutching her scorched right hand in her left, Elyse backed away from the fire, and the flames died away, leaving an ordinary log burning on the hearth, to one side, quite separate from the original fire, itself now glowing dull red once more.

'That is a very well-developed Talent you have, Elyse. Unusual. And you can Dream as well?'

'Yes, Sister.' She felt like a Novice again, completely in the power of the Sisters.

'Let me look at that hand.' She held it out. 'Well, it's

nothing serious. You were quick. You must be very careful with this fire-raising, Elyse.'

'Yes, Sister.' She was starting to get over the shock, found Sister Senior's familiar authoritative tone irritating. Whose Talent *was* it, anyway? But she was beginning to feel warm inside, too. She *could* have her Talent and Gregor as well! And the sight of the flaring log had given her the insight into how Hawk really could help to bring back the rains, or at least find out where they had gone. But she *must* show everyone that she was an important part of these new developments, not let them lock her away in the Halls once again, or send her back to the East to raise more witch babies.

'Shouldn't we talk to the Navigator and Hawk?'

'If you are ready. But are you not going to tell me your plans first?'

She shook her head. Once would be enough. And she wanted to see their faces when she spoke. 'No. Bring them in, Sister. Let me show them how useful my Talent can be.' And, she thought, maybe you'll appreciate how hasty you were in getting rid of me, too.

She sat next to Sister Senior again, where Sister Speaker had sat before, but now with her hands on the table, gazing out into the Audience Hall, not sideways at Sister Senior herself. It felt natural, comfortable. More comfortable than those hard benches out there. She didn't see the even broader smile that now passed over Sister Senior's face, before she called for the guards to bring the strangers back into the Hall.

The two strangers were brought to stand in front of the long table, clearly in an inferior position to Sister Senior and Elyse, but honoured, had they but known it, by the intimacy of the private Audience. At least, they were strangers to the Sister; to Elyse, not just their faces but their whole manner and way of standing, legs slightly apart, braced as if expecting the floor of the Hall to move like the deck of a ship, was entirely familiar. They seemed confident, happy with the situation, although Hawk's eyes bored into her. She knew, though, that this was part of their training, a result of long experience, and guessed that inwardly they must be seething with questions they wanted to ask. She had the complete advantage over them. It was a moment to be treasured.

The Navigator spoke first, addressing Sister Senior. 'My Lady, if there is any way that we can help you with your problems, we will be glad to do so, in return for your help with ours. But first we would like to know how this girl,' his eyes flicked to Elyse then back to the Sister, 'can know so much about us. Have there been other visitors from across the sea?'

'No. You are the first visitors we have had from beyond these Lands. But you must have learned, surely, during your days in Seahaven, that we in the Halls have certain powers which are not widely known elsewhere?'

'Superstition.' Hawk spat the word out. 'I mean no offence, Lady, and as a guest I would not spread the news outside, but it is quite clear how you rule this Land. You have Knowledge here, not mystic powers. You may fool your own people, but you cannot fool me. I understand the power of Knowledge, and how it can be used to fool the superstitious.'

'Yes.' Elyse spoke quietly. 'You certainly turned that to your advantage, Hawk, when you were escaping from the clutches of Ballastre. That trick with the morphic resonator, pretending you could bring down the lightning. Very neat.' The composed front of the two sailors collapsed. They turned to one another in astonishment, each clearly wondering if the other had been indiscreet, then realizing that there was no way either of them could have conveyed the information to Elyse. She continued.

'And I could discuss with you, had we but time, your strange ideas concerning the shape of the world.' Unbidden, the image of the metal egg swam into her head. Now, *there* was a mystery that Hawk might be able to help her with. But not yet. 'But these are not important. What *is* important is your obsession with fire, Hawk. An interest that I share. You seem to be good at escaping, friend Hawk; but also good at getting into situations where you need to escape. Well, here you are, trapped. You can go no further north, you say, because of the Land. But you want to continue your journey, the long way round. There is one way out of the trap. Over the White Mountains. That is where the clouds and rain come from – used to come from. We can help you on your journey, but you must take me with you over the mountains, to find out why the rain has stopped.'

'And how do you propose to travel over the mountains?' It was his last desperate attempt at calling her supposed bluff. 'Fly?'

'Of course. I know of two ways in which a man – or a woman – can fly. One is with wings, like those of your passenger, Bah-lee. One is with a skysail, like the one you used to escape from Bah-lee's people. As I said, you are a good escaper.'

She turned to the Sister. 'This is the plan that I saw in Hawk's mind, when he suddenly became so fascinated by the ceiling. To fly over the mountains, and restore the rain.' She turned back to the little man. 'Am I right?'

'Completely. There is no point in denying it. But how did you know? And can we trust you?'

'I have a Talent, Hawk. I can see things, from a distance.' No point in explaining how patchy her Talent

131

was, or that the only thing she could Dream about reliably was the *Far Trader* and her crew. Least of all that it seemed to work better from a distance than from close up. 'I have watched you since before you left the Three Islands, although I did not know until you arrived here whether you were real or not. As for trust, you have no choice but to trust us. But you have no reason to fear us, because I know all about you, and I can assure the Sisters that they have nothing to fear from you.

'I know about your secret means of navigation; I know how your ship works – well enough, I may say, to have passed some hints on to our fishermen. Best of all, I know you, all of you. I know that the Navigator is an honest man, whose word we can trust; I know that you will persuade him of the need to travel beyond the mountains, in order to satisfy your own curiosity; and I know that Captain Bryon and his crew will do anything within reason, and some things beyond reason, that their Navigator demands. So all I have to do is persuade *you*. Persuade the Hawk to fly beyond the mountains, into unknown lands; to make new discoveries; and maybe to help a suffering people along the way. Even my poor powers of persuasion should be up to that task.'

The emphasis, she knew, was just right. The Hawk of her Dreams wanted to find out new things above almost all else; he would prefer not to do harm to anyone in the process, and he had no objection to being regarded as a saviour. For the moment, he was in awe of her power, and easy to manipulate. By the time he found out how feeble her Dreaming really was, it would be too late to draw back from the adventure. In any case, she could see, he was already hooked by the idea of travelling onward with the aid of a skysail, where no ship of the sea could possibly go. She could already tell that the

Navigator was resigning himself, probably not all that unwillingly, to participating in another of the Hawk's wild schemes.

There was one last detail to slot into place, one possible objection to her own physical involvement with the adventure to overcome before it could be raised.

'There's one more thing, Hawk. Your skysail needs fire to carry it aloft.' He nodded. 'I think it may just be possible that I can help you there, as well.' She turned to Sister Senior, and smiled. The day hadn't turned out too badly, after all.

SEVEN

In spite of the fall in the river level, it was still possible to navigate the *Far Trader* a little way inland. The Little River, although much narrower than the Great River, was also much deeper, at least in its lower reaches. The steep sides of the valley, enclosing a deep river with easy access to the sea but narrow enough for easy crossing by ferry or the new bridge (still 'new' even though it had been built long before Elyse had been born) had made this the natural site for the main centre of population in all the Land. But inland, within a day's ride the valley had given way to the short stretch of plain before the foothills of the mountains, and the river spread into a wider, shallower and slower flow. Further north still, up into the hills and mountains themselves, it narrowed once again, tumbling down waterfalls and rapids impassable by any boat, let alone a sea-going ship. But Bryon would risk grounding his vessel permanently only for a much shorter journey, scarcely three days' ride from the town.

Even so, it had been worth the effort, with men working oars where they could, towing the ship from small boats, hauling on lines stretched out to the river bank, and even poling it off the river bed. It meant that they had everything that the ship could supply, in terms of tools and equipment, as well as able-bodied men, unwearied by a long hike, that much further north to establish a camp from which they could set out into the mountains.

The haul overland was grim enough to make them all appreciate the effort that the ship had saved them. The load was impressive: almost all of the finest sailcloth from the *Far Trader*, now fashioned into a skysail big enough, they hoped, to carry two people over the mountains. Bah-lee's wings, disassembled and light enough by their very nature, but awkwardly shaped, and more fragile than anyone who had only seen them soaring from a distance might expect. Food for the six hands of men — and one woman — manœuvring everything as far as possible up into the hills. And last, but by no means least, the flat metal platform and the metal fire-basket which they intended to use to build a fire that could be carried aloft with the balloon itself.

The attraction between the sun and their fire must, said Hawk, increase as they rose up closer to the sun, just as the resonance between his small spark generator and the large spark generator back in Lord Kyper's keep was stronger when the *Far Trader* was closer to the Three Islands. The idea was to attach the edges of the metal platform by ropes to the skysail, and build a fire on the platform. Of course, as the first stage in making the skysail fly they would also need a large bonfire, alongside the platform, just as Hawk had used a bonfire to make the hot air and smoke which lifted him upwards before. If they could build a fire big enough to make sufficient hot air to lift the whole thing off the ground, then the second stage of the plan would come into operation. The increasing attraction between the fire on the platform and the sun would cause it to rise faster and faster, until they damped the flames down.

There had been no time to test the idea, but Hawk was confident. Extrapolation from something he knew about — the morphic resonator — to something similar but as yet unknown was, he said, an essential step towards a true understanding of the world. It was essentially the same process of logical thought that had enabled Bah-lee's people to extrapolate the way a bird could glide into wings big enough to carry a man; or which Hawk himself had used to extrapolate the flight of a burning piece of paper into the flight of a skysail.

Elyse was less confident in the power of pure thought to make such leaps, without any practical test, but the Navigator and all his crew seemed to have supreme confidence in the Hawk, and like them she knew his record of success. Besides, it was her idea to fly over the mountains; Hawk's job was to make that fantasy practicable reality, and who was she to object to how he might choose to do it? At present, in any case, she didn't want to be seen as a dissenting voice, for her own good reasons. There had been enough muttered objections to her presence on the expedition at all, in spite of the firm insistence of both Sister Senior and the Navigator that she was a key member of the expedition – although only Sister Senior knew that she retained her power over fire, she had appointed Elyse as her personal representative on the expedition, nominal co-leader, with the Navigator, who had to accept her status if he wanted any help from the Halls later. In truth, he seemed happy enough to do so, impressed by her witch-Knowledge of his own past, and not being conditioned by his upbringing to believe implicitly that she had lost her powers. Indeed, it might be natural if he believed that the story that she no longer had those powers was no more than a political ruse on the part of the Sisters. That would certainly explain why he treated her with such respect – and she was uncomfortably aware that it was also true, even if her Dreaming did not actually give her access to his secret thoughts.

The men from Seahaven seemed to resent her most. In their view, they were willing to accept the rule of the Sisters from the Halls, because they needed their special Talents; but any woman outside the Halls (even, or perhaps *especially*, a former witch) should, very definitely, be subservient to men. The sailors were, it seemed, more or less happy to accept anything that the Navigator said was good for them, and she guessed that their encounters with the unusual on their travels had made them more responsive to new ideas. But in both camps there seemed to be a tacit assumption that the two-man skysail would be carrying Hawk and the Navigator on its flight of discovery. She had other plans, and preferred to work quietly to find a way to bring them to fruition, rather than make a nuisance of herself and create hostility towards herself.

Her opportunity came sooner than she had expected. They had set up camp on the edge of a small plateau, just below the steep rise of the cliffs that protected the White Mountains proper. This was as far north as any man had ever penetrated. The cliffs themselves were not spectacularly high, but they were sheer, with a slight overhang, and said to be unclimbable. Several foolhardy adventurers of the past had, according to legend, lost their lives trying to climb them, and nobody in the present party had any intention of testing their own skills against the curiously flat surface, which looked and felt like barren rock, but which had no trace of vegetation on its surface, not even moss, and which resisted the desultory attempts of a few of the sailors to knock lumps off for souvenirs. But nobody paid much attention to the oddness of the cliff face; what did it matter, if they had the means to fly over the cliff without even touching it? And once even a couple of men were on the top of the cliff, a rope or two, and some of the pulleys thoughtfully provided from the ship's stores, would soon see the rest of the party up there as well.

In the opposite direction, back south, the way they had come, a steep incline gave way to the rolling hills over which they had toiled, giving a superb view of the wild lands. A little way to the east, the headwaters of the Little River tumbled down from the mountains, splashing over the edge of the plateau to form a cascading succession of modest waterfalls down on to the land below. Ahead, to the north, the mountain wall itself rose into the heights. The streamer of white cloud that gave the mountains their name rolled off their peaks, which were shielded from view by the white blanket, and dipped down towards them, like another, greater waterfall, only to disappear into thin air a short distance below the peaks. And all the while a light but steady cool breeze blew their way from the cliff at the base of the mountains.

Standing in the breeze, a short distance away from the bustling activity of the camp, out of earshot of the men, the four senior members of the expedition considered the implications of this unexpected discovery.

'Well, Hawk. Your skysail cannot fly against the wind.' The Navigator didn't seem too concerned by the setback, Elyse noted. Was it just that he had faith in Hawk to pull something off? Or was he happy for an excuse to abandon the expedition? Either way, Hawk was in his element.

'But who can tell which way the winds are blowing up there?' He gestured, expansively, in the general direction of the sun.

'Who indeed? Why should they be any more assistance to us up there than they are down here?'

Hawk smiled. 'Ah, Rantor, have you learnt so little on our travels? Think. Where does wind come from?'

The Navigator turned his eyes on the Hawk, locked his gaze. Obviously, if Hawk wanted to lead him step by step, like a child, to some great new discovery, he would play the game. 'Wind? Why, it is nothing but moving air.'

'And what lies behind it?'

'More moving air. Unless the wind stops.'

'Exactly.' The little man seemed pleased with his pupil. 'There is always more air behind the winds. Now, think of what we know about the land breeze and the sea breeze. As you explained to me once, long ago, the wind blows towards the land by day, and from the land out to sea at night.'

'And you explained to me how this all has to do with the affinity of hot things for the sun, and cold things for the sea.'

'Yes. But that is not important now. It is the same wind – the same air – d'you see, moving to and fro all the time, like water slopping to and fro in a tub. First one way – sea breeze – and then the other – land breeze. There is no *new* air. Air is conserved. It is a fundamental law. Air can neither be created nor destroyed.'

Elyse could no longer hold her silence. 'But *this* breeze never changes direction.'

'No.' Hawk turned his piercing eyes on her. 'So where does it come from? It is not slopping to and fro like water in a tub. It flows steadily all the time, like a river. Where does the water in a river come from?'

It was her turn to play the part of pupil. 'Rain. From the sky.'

'Exactly. So where must the air to make this river of wind come from?' Impatient to reach the end of his explanation, Hawk answered himself. 'From above. From the sky. We cannot see it, but there must be a wind blowing towards the mountains, high up, in the warmth of the sun. When it arrives at the mountains, it cools under the shade of the cloud, and flows down the mountain side, all the way down to these cliffs, to make this breeze. Somewhere down in those hills,' he swept a hand in a vague gesture southward, 'it warms and rises again, circling endlessly. All we have to do is float our skysail along in the current.'

'And avoid getting it dashed to pieces on the rocks before we get high enough to find your river of air.'

'Yes. We must start our flight from as close to the cliff as possible, and rise swiftly enough to avoid being carried down over the edge of the plateau.'

'Will the skysail rise that fast?'

For once, Hawk seemed discomfited. 'I don't know. It depends how strongly the winds blow at different heights. How fiercely the fire burns in the basket. How strongly the fire is attracted by the sun.' He shrugged. 'I just don't know.'

Bah-lee, who had stood quietly listening to the discussion, spoke for the first time. 'Then it is fortunate, is it not, that you have a flier here who can go ahead of you, to find out all these things?'

The Navigator turned to him. 'How? We cannot lift you with the skysail, as I had hoped, until we know what we are lifting into. And you cannot soar upward without the rising breeze.'

Bah-lee shook his head. 'You still know very little about flying, Navigator. I can launch myself from the edge of this plateau, with great ease. I can fly above the hills, and if there is rising air there, I will gain height more than sufficient to fly back over your heads and towards the mountains. There, I will find which way the wind blows, and report back.'

'Or fly straight on, over to the mountains, without waiting for us.'

The flier smiled. 'You have no choice. I fly where the wind takes me. If it takes me to the mountains, then at least you will know which way to follow. If Hawk is wrong, I will be left down there in the hills, on my own. But better to lose one flier in the wild land than the two of you, I think.'

Rantor nodded. He spoke to Elyse. 'And the loss of our flier in such a way would, undoubtedly, satisfy the Sisters that we had made every effort to carry out our promise?'

Could she speak for the Sisters in accepting this gesture as sufficient? Should she insist on more effort to reach the mountain tops? What if she insisted on attempting a skysail flight, even if Bah-lee failed, and the Navigator ignored her? She nodded, weakly. 'If the flier cannot soar high enough, we must give up. But if he *does* succeed,' her voice firmed, 'then you must swear to let the skysail follow.'

'Of course.' He seemed genuinely surprised. 'I would not wish to come so far and not have a chance to learn what lies beyond. Even if Hawk would let us return, once Bah-lee has shown the way.'

So it was settled. But while Bah-lee and the Navigator began to stroll back towards the main camp, where the disassembled flier lay, Elyse stayed close by Hawk, touching him lightly on the arm to hold him back for a moment. Something he had said had been nagging away in her head.

'Hawk?'

'Yes?' Like the Navigator, he had been coolly polite to her, but no more, throughout their journey.

'Where does the rain come from? To make the rivers?'

'From the sky.' He started to turn away, to follow Rantor.

'But how does it get into the sky?' He stopped, turned back to her. Hurriedly, she went on. 'The sea level doesn't change, does it? Even with all the rivers pouring into it. I mean, would you say that sea level is conserved, like air?'

'So the water to make the rain must come from the sea, to complete the cycle ...' his voice tailed away. 'Unless the sea is infinite, of course, in which case you could add all the water you liked and the level would not change.'

'But if we live in a finite world? The inner sphere?'

'Then *everything* must be conserved. Wind, water, *everything*.' He grinned broadly at her, delighted. Suddenly, he linked his arm through hers, urging her into a brisk walk. 'Come. There is much to do to prepare the flier. But we must talk more about this. How can sea water get into the air to make clouds and rain? I suppose it must be attracted by the sun. But what stops it all rising up into the sky? Well, well, Elyse. So you think about things, too, instead of just accepting them. Or did you Dream this up?'

Bah-lee's flight was spectacular, but it was hard to describe it as a success. The launch, from the sloping edge of the plateau, was impressive enough in itself, with a man running at either wing tip to hold the frail craft steady while the flier himself ran between them, strapped into his wings. Then, the moment when he was no longer running, but had lifted his legs clear of the ground, crying to his helpers to release the wings, allowing him to float, at first scarcely a span above the ground and then, as the ground dropped away beneath him, out into space, leaving the two wing men collapsed in panting heaps on the grass. They had launched him out over the hills at midday, of course, when the heat from the Sun had long been at work drawing up air from the land below, and they watched intently as the circling flier's wings glinted in the sun as it twisted over the hills. At first it was below the watchers; then, slowly, as it circled it rose level with them, and kept on rising until they had to crane their necks backward in order to catch occasional glimpses of the flier.

At last, Bah-lee was ready. Turning out of the circle with a last flash of sunlight reflecting from his wings, the flier headed straight back towards the plateau, the sheer cliffs cutting it off from the White Mountains proper beyond; he was moving with impressive speed.

'He has caught the wind,' Elyse murmured, needlessly, to Gregor, at her side. 'There *is* a counter-current up there, or he would not be moving so fast.'

But fast as Bah-lee flew, it soon became clear to the watchers that he was losing height – losing too much height, perhaps, to have more than a slim chance of clearing the cliffs. As he passed overhead, there still seemed a chance that he might make it; but as they ran back towards the base of the cliffs, stumbling as they tried to run over the rough ground while gazing upward into the sky, it soon became clear that it was hopeless. Quite suddenly, the speed of the flier dropped, as he fell out of the counter-current and into still air below. The angle of his flight steepened, and the experienced sailors from the *Far Trader* could all project the line of his flight to the point where it must end. Approaching the cliff face, the flier was perhaps a hundred paces below the top. For a moment, it seemed as if Bah-lee, in his frustration, planned to fly straight into the sheer face. Then, the flier began to turn again, tightly, in a spectacular show of control. But Bah-lee had left it too late, either through overconfidence or in his anger at being unable to clear the cliff. Even as he turned, the wing nearest the cliff dipped suddenly, as it was caught in the down draught of cold air spilling over the top. Instinctively, as he struggled to regain control, Bah-lee turned in the direction of the dipping wing, bringing the whole wing system into the down draught. As he levelled up again, completing the turn back towards the now stationary, horrified watchers on the small plateau below, the flier seemed to be hurtling towards the ground without moving forward at all; then, as he emerged from the stream of descending air the front of the wings lifted abruptly as the rear section alone took the full force of the falling air. The flier soared upwards almost vertically for a few span, then the wings flipped forward and pitched him straight down on to the ground below.

When they reached Bah-lee, he was lying on his side in the wreckage of a pair of wings that clearly would not fly again, trying to raise himself on to his right elbow, picking at the harness with his left hand. Blood spread from a head wound, and he appeared to have lost at least one tooth in the impact. But he was moving, and mumbling through damaged lips.

Elyse, light on her feet and toughened by her recent travels, was surprised to be beaten to Bah-lee's side by Hawk, who cradled his injured companion's head in his arm, bending close to listen to his words.

'No problem. Plenty of current, if you keep high. Better for a skysail than wings.' He tried to grin, coughed and spat out what seemed to be another tooth. His eyes closed, then opened again. His left hand reached for Elyse's arm. 'But listen. I could see over the top, before I reached the cliff. There is no land there. No trees. No grass. No land. It shines like metal in the sun. But there is no land.' His grip relaxed, as he repeatedly muttered 'no land', and closed his eyes.

Elyse scarcely paid any attention to the words. She was busy feeling Bah-lee's limbs, and then gently probing at his chest, using the limited healing skills she had learnt in the Halls.

'Nothing broken, except perhaps a rib, here. But the head . . .' she reached forward and wiped at the blood on his forehead with the sleeve of her robe. It was an ugly gash, surrounded by bruising and already swelling noticeably. As well as the missing teeth, there seemed to be something wrong with the shape of the flier's nose, and he was surely going to have a spectacular pair of black eyes. But as far as she could tell, there was nothing more serious. And he had certainly been talking quite clearly, just before passing into a healing sleep. He'd probably survive. But what had he been saying?

Hawk, having passed Bah-lee into the care of several pairs of gentle hands that were busy disentangling him from the wreckage, straightening his limbs, cushioning his head with a bundle of clothing and cleaning his wounds, sat back on his haunches, looking up at the Navigator, who stood slightly aloof from the bustle.

'Well?'

'No problem, Navigator. His very words. The counter-current is strong, and blows all the way. He just lost height too quickly, a problem which we will not have to face.'

'There's more, Hawk. I see it in your eyes.'

'Yes.' Hawk glanced at Elyse, then back to the Navigator. 'No trees, no grass. A land of metal, he said. Although he was scarce speaking sense by then.'

'Metal or not, Hawk, that's where we are going. And without delay. Prepare the skysail.'

His words triggered a flurry of hasty activity amongst the men, who had clearly not been expecting this. Elyse was equally startled. Surely this was not the time? Then, as she watched the initially confused bustle settle into an orderly pattern of activity around the ready prepared firewood, she understood. It was *exactly* the right time. It would make no difference to Bah-lee's recovery whether the skysail flew or not, and the Navigator wanted his men to be active, not brooding over the failure of Bah-lee's flight. Get them to work on familiar things, and the skysail aloft, before anyone decided that the whole expedition was cursed by bad luck, or that it was working against fate to attempt to reach the heights above the cliff, or something. Wait until tomorrow, and if Bah-lee showed no signs of recovery such ideas might spread; while if they went now, whether or not the flier recovered the expedition would be moving on. Although, even with that acknowledged, it was getting late in the day for a flight into the unknown. If they made it, they'd surely have to wait out the night up there, alone, before the rope hoist could be set up. She shivered at the thought.

But things were moving too quickly. The skysail and fire were being prepared, with the Navigator and Hawk ready to mount the platform, stacked around with wood, the brazier already glowing in the middle. And if they were successful on this flight, they'd be sure to follow the same plan later, so she might never get her own chance to fly, closer to the mountains. While if they were unsuccessful, *nobody* would get another chance.

Uncertain how to respond, she backed away from the bustle of activity part way towards the edge of the plateau. The bonfire, flames leaping impressively, was close to the base of the cliff, but far enough away to be out of the down draught. The flames and smoke licked outwards, away from the cliff, in the direction that the skysail would inevitably follow as it rose from the ground.

She watched the technique, fascinated. It was like seeing one of her Dreams come to life. The same arrangement of ropes and strong poles to lift the mouth of the skysail over the hot, rising smoke from the fire, the same swelling belly of the skysail itself beginning to lift from the ground and sway over the leaping flames.

Gregor had followed her away from the bonfire. Silently, he put his arm around her shoulders. She knew that he understood how much she wanted to be the one to venture forward, into unknown territory, and bring back the water to the Land. He would never stop her, of that she was certain, although she in turn understood his own wish to keep her by his side.

Suddenly, everything was ready. Hawk and the Navigator were on the platform, which was lifting clear of the ground, held now by the last two ropes. Men below were throwing chunks of timber up to them, to feed the brazier without resorting, yet, to the wood stacked around the platform. It was important, Hawk had explained, to keep the fire provided with fresh wood, making ample smoke to lift the skysail. Then, they were free. As expected, the skysail began to rise swiftly once it was released, and at the same time to move out from the base of the cliffs, heading directly over her head. But then, instead of gaining more height, it was pressed back down, as if by a giant hand. It could only be the down draught, extending further out from the cliff, a little above the ground, than Hawk had realized. They were going to crash!

Released from Gregor's grip, she ran, almost under the shadow of the bobbing skysail. For a moment, it started to lift again, then it was blown almost on its side, spilling the all-important hot smoke from its mouth. It lurched downward again, smashing through some scrubby trees towards the edge of the plateau, bouncing the platform towards an upwardly jutting finger of rock. The Navigator was leaning over the side of the platform, attending to some problem in the rigging of the skysail, when it hit the rock. He tumbled, seemingly as slowly as if he were floating through water, bringing one of the long ropes looping down with his body. Everything seemed to be moving very slowly around Elyse. She had all the time in the world to notice how the Navigator fell, grasping for the rope, hands slipping past it, somersaulting, landing on his back, winded, in a patch of bushes. She saw the skysail lurching over the edge of the plateau, barely maintaining height even without the weight of the Navigator, the rope trailing behind it. She felt herself running, jumping, seemingly flying, catching hold of the rope, slipping a little, then grasping it with both hands, winding her legs around it, being carried out, swaying underneath the metal platform, Hawk's face looking down from above.

They were losing height. The ground below was dropping away faster than they were falling, but they were still falling. She closed her eyes, conjured up an image of the glowing fire in the brazier. An image of intense fire, wood burning furiously to make glowing charcoal, heat spreading in all directions. She clung on to the rope with all her limbs.

It seemed nothing happened. There was no wind any more, just silence, and the rope, and a picture in her mind of glowing fire. Of course, something in her head seemed to say, that was wrong. Hawk wanted smoke, not glowing charcoal. But her Talent wasn't good at making smoke any more, just at making things burn fiercely. Too bad. She was preparing herself for the inevitable impact with the trees, hunching her legs up under her body, when a voice broke into her train of thought. It was Hawk, calling from no more than four or five span over her head, making her open her eyes again.

'How did you do that?' He seemed unruffled, interested by the developments, but not bothered by his predicament.

She looked down. They were well above the hills, and the trees covering the hillsides seemed to be getting smaller as they rose higher into the sky. His voice continued, as casual as if he were back in the Halls, or on board the *Far Trader*, or even in Lord Kyper's castle. 'It's all wrong, of course. No smoke. But it seems to work very well. Perhaps the glowing charcoal has a greater affinity for the glowing sun than mere smoke can ever have.'

She looked up. Hawk was leaning nonchalantly on the wooden side of the platform.

'Put more wood on the fire,' she managed to utter between teeth that seemed reluctant to part. 'I'll make it burn, but you've got to put it there first. Then help me up.'

She shut her eyes again, concentrating on the image of fire. So he *did* want glowing charcoal. She'd make it glow, all right. She felt a brief tug on the rope, and opened her eyes once more. Then, keeping her gaze fixed upward on Hawk's grinning face, she crept her way upward until he could grasp her hands, helping her over the low side and on to the platform itself. The fire was glowing almost white, the brazier itself was cherry red, sagging under its own weight in the heat. It was uncomfortably hot on the little platform, hemmed in by the wood supplies that were being rapidly depleted as Hawk continued to toss more logs into the hungry fire, while speaking to her in short sentences.

'I think you can leave it, now. Let it burn naturally. It is your doing?' She nodded. 'Don't bother explaining. Look. We're on our way.'

She looked over the edge. They were now much higher, well above the plateau itself. She could see, almost directly below, the rocky outcrop where the skysail had hit, a cluster of figures around what could only be the Navigator himself, standing on the highest point, looking up at them. Further ahead, the bonfire still sent a plume of smoke trailing out across the plateau, and another group of figures could be discerned clustered around Bah-lee. Further north still, seemingly rapidly approaching them as they hung motionless in the air, were the cliffs. The skysail was higher than the clifftop! Higher, she was sure, than Bah-lee had reached on his flight. Moving in the counter-current – no winds blowing past them, because they were moving as fast as the wind itself, exactly where they wanted to go. She turned back to Hawk, hugged him with delight.

'I *knew* my fire Talent would be useful.' She let go, looked out again, decided they were losing height, picked up some wood from the much diminished pile and added it to the brazier. Hawk followed suit.

'So it wasn't the fire burning brighter as it got closer to the sun.' He shook his head, ruefully. 'But since it flared up as soon as you latched on to that rope, it took no great power of deduction to work out who was responsible. A neat trick, though. Can you do it any time?'

'Not like that. It needs some strong feeling to set it off. Fear, usually.' She laughed. 'But I can make it burn a little brighter than it is now, if you want to be sure of getting over those cliffs.'

He nodded towards the fast approaching cliffs. 'Not just yet.' His voice took on the contemplative quality she knew so well from her Dreams. 'It's interesting, is it not, how the mountains seem to be moving towards us, rather than us being carried towards the mountains. Relativity of motion. Did we really sail here from the Three Islands, or did the Three Islands sail away and leave us floating in the sea, waiting for your Land to sail past?'

'And is the skysail falling down towards the ground, or is the ground rushing up to meet us? Either way, Hawk, there's a nasty bump at the end of it.'

The slight exaggeration jolted him out of his incipient day-dream, as she intended. He glanced below, checking that they were actually just about maintaining a steady height, then forward again. 'Well, put the rest of the wood on, in that case. Then see what you can do about making it burn brightly. Rantor is going to be sore that he is missing this, but it has to be said, if he was here and you were not, we wouldn't be here at all, if you follow me.'

'I follow.' They piled the remaining wood on the flames, then she stood, gazing intently into the heart of the fire, willing it to burn more brightly. The flames leapt up from the fresh logs, carrying smoke into the gaping mouth of the skysail above. She became aware of Hawk's gaze, watching her as intently as she watched the flames, and turned away, looking out to see the effect of her efforts. They had certainly gained height once again, and would easily pass over the cliffs, into the land beyond. But what did lie beyond the cliffs?

'Look.' Hawk turned to follow her pointing arm. The land beyond the clifftop did indeed glitter, like metal in the sunlight. There were no trees, no grass. But there was something moving, ponderously, from the base of the mountains out towards the clifftop. To be visible so far away, it had to be huge – a moving castle. And yet there was something very odd about the appearance of the mountains themselves, from up here. They looked almost like a model, a child's toy, like a carved model of a boat seen close up, rather than a real ship seen far away. Like *pretend* mountains. She shook her head. It must be the strange angle they were looking from, so high up. She looked straight down. But not so high up, after all. They were already over the clifftop, now sinking rapidly towards the strange, flat plain below. She turned back to the fire, leaving Hawk gazing out towards the thing moving towards them from the mountains. The remaining embers flared brightly as she concentrated on them, but there was little heat left for them to give.

'Hawk!' He ignored her, still gazing into the distance. 'Hawk! We have no more fire!'

'It isn't important. We don't need it, now.'

'How do we land?'

He turned back to her, smiled. 'I don't know. I've never done this before. Better hold on tight to something.'

Following his example, she grabbed hold of two of the ropes that joined the platform to the skysail. Idiot! Of course, the only time he'd ever flown before, he'd simply dropped into the sea at the end of the flight. She'd seen it all, in her Dreams. But whatever that shiny surface rushing up to meet them was, it certainly wasn't water. They were going to hit, and hard.

She had time to notice that they were moving back towards the clifftop, obviously caught, now, in the downward flow of cold air, and opened her mouth to say something that would wipe the grin off his face, but her teeth were snapped shut by the impact. Everything tipped sideways, and she lost her grip with her right hand, clinging only by the left as they bumped over the surface. The skysail settled to one side, spilling warmth from its mouth, dragging them a little further, then stopping. She let go with her left hand, too, and fell forward on all fours on to the ground – if it was ground – below. She looked up, on a scene that might belong in one of her Dreams, not in the real world. Hawk was lying on his back, laughing. There was a tangle of ropes around the deflating skysail. Beyond, the cliff edge seemed far too close for comfort, and the steady breeze seemed to be urging her towards it, even now; but turning her head she could see a flat, featureless plain stretching to the base of mountains that seemed almost close enough to touch, and strangely out of proportion. Then, the sun went out.

They sat by a small fire, kindled from the embers in the brazier. Elyse was feeding pieces of wood, broken off from the sides of the skysail platform, into the flames, and trying hard not to encourage them to burn too brightly. To that end, she was careful not to look into the fire, but out into the darkness. Hawk, of course, was talking.

'With just one rope in place, secure at this end, some of our sailors will come swarming up in no time. They're used to ropes. And once they rig up a pulley, with a travelling block –'

'What's that light?'

He turned. There was a bright light, approaching swiftly from the direction of the mountains. Rather, two bright lights – Elyse stood to gauge them better – perhaps a little higher above the ground than her own head, spaced some distance apart, producing a double pool of reflection on the metallic surface of the plain, still approaching, and now accompanied by a faint hum. Hawk stood as well, and she moved alongside him, instinctively, her head just overtopping his. Neither of them made any attempt to flee. Where was there to flee to? Besides, they had come here to explore the unknown, and this was certainly the unknown.

The lights were moving, she realized, to pass close by them. The shifting angle suddenly gave her an idea of the proximity of the things – very close – and their spacing, about five paces apart. The quietness of their approach, and the lack of any reference points, had given a false impression of distance. Then, in a rush, they swept past, and stopped. She could see, blinking as her eyes adjusted, that they were mounted on the front of a kind of travelling box, about as big as a large room, floating just above the surface of the plain. The double pool of light was now centred on the wreckage of the skysail, as if the box were a living creature looking at it. Then it turned, the whole floating room turning gently, like a leaf twisting in the breeze, until the pool of light crept over them, still standing, side by side, near the flickering embers of the fire.

'I don't understand why it floats.'

'What?' She was still not entirely used to the way Hawk's mind worked.

'That box. It's made of metal, I believe. So it should be attracted to the metal surface we are standing on. And yet it floats. I don't understand.'

'*Please speak some more.*'

The Voice came from the box. They were both too startled to respond immediately.

'*Please speak in turn, for identification purposes.*'

'Who are you?' Hawk recovered first.

'What do you want me to say?' Elyse paid more attention to the request.

'*Please speak in turn. The female first. Tell me where you come from.*'

'I come from Seahaven. From the Halls.' She gained in confidence at the thought. 'I represent the Sisters, and I am the co-leader of this expedition. We have come –'

'Enough. Thank you. I have confirmed the dialect. A Sister, from the Halls, in Seahaven. Now the male.'

'I come from the Three Islands, in the service of Lord Kyper, but that is not important now. How do you float like that? Surely the attraction of similarities would stick you to the surface? Do you come from the mountains? How far is it? Something doesn't seem to be right about the appearance –'

So he'd noticed, too! But Hawk's stream of questions was cut off as abruptly as she had been.

'Enough. Thank you. The dialect is unfamiliar. Where are these Three Islands?'

'Far to the south. Many hands of days.'

Elyse noticed that Hawk was careful not to be too precise.

'In the southern hemisphere, perhaps. My sensors are widely scattered, there.'

She broke in. 'The southern hemisphere. Part of a sphere. The inner sphere?'

'You seem well-informed, Sister from the Halls. Surprisingly well-informed. Your companion is no less surprising. A traveller from the far south. And there is this balloon to explain.' Balloon? What in the Land was a balloon? The Voice continued. 'I cannot calculate how, using wood alone, you could generate enough heat to sustain altitude in the jet stream for sufficient time. None of this matches my projections.' She shook her head, trying to make some sense out of the words. It sounded as if the Voice was explaining something, but what she couldn't fathom. 'But at least you are here, and it is quite clear that you have arrived through your own efforts, and those of other humans, unaided by forbidden knowledge. I think I can stretch a point, and offer you a ride back to the Bridge, if you wish.'

'Bridge? What bridge?' Hawk's question coincided with the appearance of a crack in the side of the box, a crack which widened to reveal a small room behind – much smaller than the outer dimensions of the box – with a low couch on one side and a blank glass window at the other.

'*You think of the Bridge as the mountains. You are right, it is not as far away as it seems from below the cliff.*' So the Voice hadn't forgotten their questions. '*The mountains are largely a holographic projection designed to give a false perspective suggesting great distance, to discourage visitors.*' Once again, the explanation was gobbledegook. '*The Bridge is the control and navigation centre of the ship.*' Ship? What ship? The Voice's answers were more confusing than its questions. '*The North Pole is arbitrarily regarded as the bow of the ship, although of course the ship, as you recognize, is spherically symmetrical. I can take you there in a few minutes, and show you the stars, if you like. And on the way I can answer more of your questions.*'

'What about our companions? I cannot leave until the Navigator has scaled the cliff.'

'And what about the drought? The people of the Land need water. I cannot leave until I am sure you intend to help us.'

'*Interesting.*' The Voice paused. '*An unfamiliar sensation, but satisfying, after all this time. You are quite right, of course. I cannot force you to do anything. Within certain limits, you are certainly in command, Sister, as co-leader of the expedition.*' She noticed a subtle change in the Voice, no longer impersonal, as it switched from addressing her, in language that would not have been out of place in the Halls themselves, to addressing Hawk, in dialect more like that of the sailors. '*And we can easily bring your Navigator up as soon as it gets light. I'd rather not bring the dawn forward, if you don't mind, since it would cause so much confusion throughout the ship. But we can wait here for a few hours, and I can answer some of your questions. I would certainly like to talk with another navigator again.'*

'What about the drought?'

'I have not forgotten. I rarely forget. I have been looking into the reference while we were talking. There are difficulties with the main drive, and I need the reaction mass for imminent manœuvring using the secondary system. But maybe I have indeed been a little thoughtless in arranging for this. Everything will average out over the next two seasons, leaving normal weather patterns with a slightly lower sea level. But I can bring the rain forward a little, if you wish.'

'I do.' Elyse hadn't missed the reference to her being in command. She didn't know what this talking box was capable of, and she didn't know if it really would obey her. But what had she to lose? 'I want normal rainfall throughout the Land, this season. And I want the Great River back to its normal flow, but gradually, not all in a rush.'

'And while I am attending to that, and we are waiting for dawn, would you like to sit while I answer your questions?'

'We'll sit, but out here.' Hawk suited his actions to his words; she followed suit. It made sense. More sense than the Voice. When she could understand the words, they still didn't add up. How could it attend to the rainfall while it stayed here talking to them? Once inside that box, anything could happen to her and Hawk. Not, she reminded herself, that it couldn't happen to them out here, anyway. But it felt as if they were more in control of things.

'In that case, I'll have to skip the film show for now. I think you would have enjoyed it. Very educational. But I'm getting used to human speech patterns now, and I'll do my best anyway.

'You have asked just one question that I have not yet answered. How does this vehicle float above the surface. Are you familiar with magnetism?'

Elyse and Hawk looked at each other in the firelight, shrugged. Hawk spoke for them both. 'No.'

'Very well. You spoke of the attraction of similarities. Can you give me an example?'

'Hot smoke, rising to greet the sun.'

'Interesting. Well, metals obey a law which is precisely the reverse of this. You might call it the repulsion of similarities. Using electricity, it is possible to make two — ah — flavours of metal. Opposites attract, similar varieties repel. These magnetic flavours are induced in the metal of the vehicle, and in the surface below. So, it floats.'

It meant nothing to Elyse, but Hawk, as ever, had latched on to something hidden in the noise.

'And what is electricity?'

'Like lightning, but controlled, constrained to flow in wires. But, of course, you have no experience of that, either. Let me explain . . .'

'But I do!' He was triumphant. 'We use controlled lightning to navigate, when we are closer to the Three Islands. Let me explain.'

And he was off, lost in discussion with the disembodied Voice. A discussion that ranged far, from the workings of Hawk's morphic resonator, which seemed of great interest to the Voice, to the notion of stars, other suns, but outside the sphere in which their world was contained. That didn't seem too difficult to grasp; she would like to see these stars, when the Navigator arrived and they could move on to the Bridge that the Voice talked about. Even the prospect of an infinitely large world *outside* the world, scattered with *stars*, and presumably with other worlds, seemed like a more or less straight-forward development from all that she had learned, from sharing Hawk's experiences in her Dreams, about the nature of infinity. If they lived in the inner sphere, obviously it made sense, once you thought about it, that there must be something *outside*, beneath their feet. It couldn't be solid rock all the way to infinity, could it?

But then came the incomprehensible part.

'No, Hawk.' The Voice was insistent, tireless, even though he had grown hoarse with question and answer, and it must surely be close to dawn by now. *'There are no other worlds like this, as far as I am aware. The other worlds are spherical, but solid. They have atmosphere, some of them, on the outside. And life, on a few of them, also on the outside.'*

She broke in. 'But how? Why doesn't everything fall out, into the space between the stars?'

'Because the natural tendency is not for things to fall outward, but to fall inward. It really is rather like your attraction of similarities. Things fall towards the centre.'

'That's nonsense. How could we live inside a sphere, if things fall towards the centre? Why don't we fall into the sun? Because things naturally fall outwards, of course.'

'No.' There was a pause. *'I had intended to wait a little longer, but it is all one story. It is unnatural for things to fall outward. Just as it is unnatural for a floating object to move against the wind.'*

'But that is simply a sailor's trick. I learnt it from watching the *Far Trader*.'

Hawk was quicker than her, this time. 'He means that

a ship can do unnatural things because people build it to do unnatural things. He means that in our world things fall outward because our world has been *built* that way.'

The words came back, sharp and clear in her memory. *Now* they made sense, after a fashion. 'And "the Bridge is the control and navigation centre of the ship". He means that this whole world is a *ship*. And we are passengers. Why? Where are we going? Where is the crew?'

'Yes. Well, I am the crew, now. There were humans, in command, living in the mountains, on the Bridge. Too few. They died out, you see, and left me in charge. It seemed the best solution, after all. Nobody wanted to interfere with the passengers, and there was little enough for any human to do, after the first couple of centuries. I don't think they really believed in the voyage, at the end.'

'What is a century? How long has this voyage been going on?' The half-understood explanation had raised an awful suspicion in her mind.

'A century is a hundred years. A hundred seasonal cycles. A double hand of double hands. Not quite the same as a hundred cycles of your seasons; about ten per cent longer. A thousand years is a double hand of centuries. In terms of your seasonal cycle, the voyage has now been under way for four thousand, three hundred and ninety two years, eighty five days.'

'Four lots of a double hand tripled?' Even Hawk's voice shook a little at the thought. It certainly put the voyage of the *Far Trader* in a different perspective. A journey four thousand years long, carrying passengers who lived, loved and died without ever knowing that they were on a journey. Like the rats that infested the bilges of the *Far Trader*. 'But why?'

'To escape. The sun your ancestors knew, the sun that warmed the planet on which humans first appeared,

became unstable. There were colonies, in orbit around that sun. People living in habitats, artificial worlds much smaller than this ship. They conceived the idea of escape. They built this ship from the rocks that orbit among the planets. A self-sustaining life support system, with myself to oversee the ecology and a small human crew. The passengers – the first generation – knew that they would never live to see the end of the voyage. They chose mind wipe, starting new, simpler lives within the ship. Only their many-times grandchildren would ever walk on the surface of another planet.'

'But everything they knew has been lost.' Elyse, brought up in the Halls, perceived the loss of Knowledge more acutely than the loss of a planet, something she had no experience of.

'No, Sister. Not lost. I have all the information in store, ready to educate the pioneers when we reach a new world. I can show you everything you wish to see, now that you have found me. And I would welcome your guidance.'

'On what?'

'There is a possible new home within range of my sensors. It is the thirty-seventh possible planet that I have investigated since the voyage began. Twenty-three did not meet environmental specifications. Eight showed signs of intelligent life. Five showed no signs of life at all. The latest candidate is marginal. Nitrogen/oxygen atmosphere, gravity 0.8, surface seventy per cent ocean, well-developed ecosystem, but the probe was destroyed shortly after landing. Possibly by intelligent beings. And there is a fault in the main drive. We can reach the system, comfortably. If necessary, I can use the secondary drive – the reaction mass from your ocean. But if we enter orbit, and if the main drive cannot be brought back to full function, we cannot move on, even if there is intelligence. The situation calls for a human decision.'

'What's wrong with intelligence?' She picked on the one item in the litany that she thought she understood.

'My original programming calls for settlement on an uninhabited world. The risk of conflict was deemed undesirable.'

'But if we tell you to, you will land us there anyway?'

'It would be uncomfortable for me to override the instructions. But in the circumstances, a human decision would tip the balance.'

'When must we decide?' Hawk, experienced in the problems of a long voyage, cut to the heart of the matter.

'Within the next month – thirty days – three double hands of days.'

'So soon?' Elyse was furious. 'Why didn't you tell us sooner?'

'I was forbidden. The last Commander imposed some very restrictive commands on me, strengthening my original programming. Not to interfere with the passengers, until the voyage was complete, unless passengers found me unaided, or achieved a level of technology which made my discovery inevitable. Or unless there was an emergency.'

'And isn't this an emergency?'

'No. An emergency is a fault that threatens the life support systems. Even without the main drive, life would not be threatened.'

'But the voyage would never end.'

'Yes.'

'And if we don't take the chance to visit this new world?'

'We can fly by the system on a gravity-assist trajectory, with minimal use of reaction mass for the secondary drive. The next target system will be reached in one hundred and twenty-seven years. Even if the main drive fails completely, we have enough reaction mass to enter orbit there.'

'And beyond that?' She was beginning to get a better grasp of the meaning of infinity, even if half the words in the Voice's statements still made no sense.

'I have eighty-three further target systems within range in a cone of accessible trajectories extending from our present position. There are twelve exploration probes still functional out of twenty originals. Life support systems are good for at least another five thousand years, extrapolating present trends in wear and tear. No basis, as you see, for an emergency entry into closed orbit.'

'But we would miss it. And our children, and our many-times grandchildren. As if Hawk, and the Navigator, and all their companions had never left the Three Islands, but stayed there for ever, imagining that that was all the world.' She was thinking, this could be the end of a story. We can tell this thing, this Voice, to carry on, we can go home, the rains will return, everything will be as it was. Or it can be the beginning of everything. We can tell it to halt this voyage through infinity, we can find a new world, we can walk – she shivered at the thought – outside. In spite of the shiver, Elyse knew that she preferred beginnings to endings.

'And if we end this voyage,' Hawk spoke as if he had read her mind, 'we may find trouble, as we did with Bahlee's people; or we may find friends, like yourself. But we would certainly learn more about the world outside, where many suns float in the sky and things fall inward to the centre.'

'Do we have the authority to command a landing?' She wanted to be certain.

'Not yet,' the Voice responded. '*I am required to give you full information on which to base a decision. I can only do that from the Bridge. But since you have found me by yourselves, and the diagnostic tests I have been running show you to be sane, once you have full information I will obey. I can only override if you suggest a course of action which clearly endangers the passengers' lives. Entering orbit – landing, as you put it – would not do that.*'

'It is not a decision we can make without the aid of the Navigator.' But she already knew what *her* decision would be, and she had little doubt about the Navigator, either. She knew his story, after all, better than anyone except Rantor himself. What a wonderful new story *this* would be to tell her own children, and her grandchildren, if all went well.

'*Of course. It will be interesting to discuss the possibilities with another Navigator.*' There was a pause. Then the Voice spoke again. '*Dawn isn't due for another seventeen minutes. About a thousand heartbeats. But if you wish, I don't believe any great harm would be done, just this once, if I brought it forward a little. Then we could get on with helping your Navigator up the cliff.*'

'Can you really do that?' Hawk's voice expressed his delight at the prospect. Elyse was thinking, Dawn, how appropriate, the symbol of a new beginning.

'Oh yes. If the Sister wishes.'

She looked at Hawk across the faint glow of the embers of their fire. The temptation was irresistible, even if it would hasten things only a little. Her story started to shape itself in her mind, the way she would one day tell it, to her grandchildren, around the fire on the *outside* of their new home. In the beginning, she thought, there was the Voice; and then . . . 'Yes,' she said. 'Let there be light.' And there was light.

EPILOGUE

In the depths of space, but not far from a single bright star, the sphere floated in blackness. A patient observer would have been able to tell, after careful watching, that the sphere was moving on a course that would take it close by the bright star. Such an observer would also have noted the way that the sphere rotated, orienting itself in space so that it pointed – if so uniform an object could be said to point – in a particular direction. Once settled in its preferred orientation, the sphere began, as an acute observer would have been able to tell, to slow its motion relative to the bright star. And, as the slowing sphere entered the planetary system around the star, a jet of material, which spectroscopic analysis would have revealed to be essentially water, rapidly being broken down into its component hydrogen and oxygen atoms by the ultraviolet radiation from the star, might have been seen emerging from an unsuspected orifice, slowing the sphere further and pushing it into an orbit from which it would never escape. But, of course, there was no intelligent being around to notice any of this, far from the surface of any of the nine planets orbiting that star.

**Exploring New Realms
in Science Fiction/Fantasy Adventure**

BATMAN™ IS BACK IN ACTION!

Batman™: To Stalk a Specter
by Simon Hawke

Gotham City Blackmailed!

Drug Lord Caught by U.S. Commandos! Desiderio Garcia to Stand Trial in the U.S.! The headlines – and the authorities – are jubilant, but not for long. For Garcia has a deadly would-be rescuer: the superassassin known as Specter. And Specter's reign of havoc and horror has already begun. The people of Gotham City are held hostage and destined to die by the thousands unless Garcia is freed. The people's only hope lies with Batman's bold and dangerous plan. In a war with only one winner and one survivor, he's going to make himself the archkiller's target, matching his enemy weapon for weapon, deception for deception – and with good for evil!

BATMAN™ CREATED BY BOB KANE

Exploring New Realms
in Science Fiction/Fantasy Adventure

Titles already published or in preparation:

Echoes of the Fourth Magic by R. A. Salvatore

When a U.S. submarine set out from Miami and was drawn off-course by the murderous magic of the Devil's Triangle, Officer Jeff DelGiudice survived the terrifying plunge through the realms. But his good fortune had a shocking consequence. He found himself stranded in a strange world awaiting its redeemer. Here four survivors ruled the corner of the once-great Earth with the ways of white magic ... until one of them tasted the ecstasy of evil. Thalasi, Warlock of Darkness, had amassed an army to let loose death and chaos, and only the hero promised in the guardians' legends can defeat such power. Now Jeff must face his destiny — in a dangerous, wondrous quest to lead humankind's children back to the realms of Light.

The Earthsea Trilogy by Ursula Le Guin
Wizard of Earthsea · The Tombs of Atuan
The Farthest Shore

As long ago as forever and as far away as Selidor, there lived the dragonlord and Archmage, Sparrowhawk, the greatest of the great wizards — he who, when still a youth, met with the evil shadow-beast; he who later brought back the Ring of Erreth-Akbe from the Tombs of Atuan; and he who, as an old man, rode the mighty dragon Kalessin back from the land of the dead. And then, the legends say, Sparrowhawk entered his boat, *Lookfar*, turned his back on land, and without wind or sail or oar moved westward over sea and out of sight.